Green-eyed Monster

"Too famous, Longarm. You were just too famous and now I'm going to become famous, too."

"Your fame will last about as long as it takes you to drop through the trapdoor and dance at the end of a hangman's rope."

"We'll just see about that, Longarm. I've got a hunch that I'm going to get away with killing both of you."

"You know that's not going to happen."

"All I know is that putting a bullet in your belly is going to be something I'll enjoy," Pittman grated, the gun lifting slightly in his steady hand.

"Hold on!" Longarm said. "Maybe . . ."

"Shut up and die like a man!" Pittman chuckled.

"You've been drinking. Maybe I can get Marshal Vail to . . ."

"He's dead, you dumb bastard. I just told you I shot him in his damned bed."

"Billy is strong. Maybe he's going to make it."

"He *won't* make it. And the only reason you're still alive is that I wanted you to know who killed your friend and why," Eli Pittman snarled, cocking back the hammer of his gun. "If it's any consolation, I'm sure the town will give you and Billy one hell of a grand funeral."

Longarm was standing two feet in front of his second-story window and that frosted pane of glass offered him the only chance he had at living, so he twisted and dove for the window just as the gun in Pittman's fist belched fire and lead . . .

TABOR EVANS

LONGARM

AND THE
RUNAWAY NURSE

JOVE BOOKS, NEW YORK

THE BERKLEY PUBLISHING GROUP
Published by the Penguin Group
Penguin Group (USA) Inc.
375 Hudson Street, New York, New York 10014, USA
Penguin Group (Canada), 90 Eglinton Avenue East, Suite 700, Toronto, Ontario M4P 2Y3, Canada
(a division of Pearson Penguin Canada Inc.)
Penguin Books Ltd., 80 Strand, London WC2R 0RL, England
Penguin Group Ireland, 25 St. Stephen's Green, Dublin 2, Ireland (a division of Penguin Books Ltd.)
Penguin Group (Australia), 250 Camberwell Road, Camberwell, Victoria 3124, Australia
(a division of Pearson Australia Group Pty. Ltd.)
Penguin Books India Pvt. Ltd., 11 Community Centre, Panchsheel Park, New Delhi—110 017, India
Penguin Group (NZ), 67 Apollo Drive, Rosedale, Auckland 0632, New Zealand
(a division of Pearson New Zealand Ltd.)
Penguin Books (South Africa) (Pty.) Ltd., 24 Sturdee Avenue, Rosebank, Johannesburg 2196,
South Africa

Penguin Books Ltd., Registered Offices: 80 Strand, London WC2R 0RL, England

This is a work of fiction. Names, characters, places, and incidents either are the product of the author's imagination or are used fictitiously, and any resemblance to actual persons, living or dead, business establishments, events, or locales is entirely coincidental.

LONGARM AND THE RUNAWAY NURSE

A Jove Book / published by arrangement with the author

PRINTING HISTORY
Jove edition / August 2011

Copyright © 2011 by Penguin Group (USA) Inc.
Cover illustration by Milo Sinovcic.

ISBN: 978-0-515-14972-2

JOVE®
Jove Books are published by The Berkley Publishing Group,
a division of Penguin Group (USA) Inc.,
375 Hudson Street, New York, New York 10014.
JOVE® is a registered trademark of Penguin Group (USA) Inc.
The "J" design is a trademark of Penguin Group (USA) Inc.

PRINTED IN THE UNITED STATES OF AMERICA

10 9 8 7 6 5 4 3 2 1

Chapter 1

Deputy United States Marshal Custis Long awoke to the sound of someone hammering frantically on his second-floor apartment's door. He sat up, and in the moonlight that streamed through his window, he reached for his fine pocket watch.

"It's four o'clock on Sunday morning," he muttered.

"Marshal!" a voice shouted. "Wake up and unlock the door!"

Longarm kicked his long legs out from under the covers and used his palms to grind the sleep from his eyes. He was not a man to panic, and so he pulled on a pair of long underwear and yelled, "Who the hell wants me at this hour on a Sunday morning?"

"It's Deputy United States Marshal Eli Pittman! Something terrible has happened!"

Longarm jumped up from the bed, placed his gun back on the nightstand, and stumbled to unlock the door. He had recognized Pittman's excited voice, and although he barely knew the newly hired lawman, he figured this must be very important news to arrive at this hour.

He unbolted his door, and there was the deputy marshal standing in the hallway with a gun in his hand. In the lamplight Longarm could see that Pittman's eyes were wild, and the lawman reeked of bad whiskey.

"What's wrong?" Longarm asked.

Pittman swallowed hard. "Our boss, Billy Vail, has just been shot."

"How did it happen and how bad is he?" Billy Vail was not only Longarm's boss, he was his best friend.

Pittman shook his head back and forth as if he were trying to throw off a nightmare. "Marshal Vail just took a bullet in the belly and I expect that he'll most likely die."

The breath exploded from Longarm's lungs. "Where is Billy right now?"

"They took him to the hospital. He's in real bad shape. A lot of pain. He was calling for you when I left on the run. He gave me your address and I got here just as fast as my legs would carry me."

"Do they know who shot him?" Longarm asked, whirling around to get his clothes, boots, and flat-brimmed hat.

"Not yet . . . but *you* do."

It was dark in the bedroom and very cold. This was November and the night temperatures were dropping into the mid-twenties. Longarm could see his breath as he grabbed his pants and began to pull them on, saying, "Eli, how the hell would *I* know who just shot Billy?"

"Because I'm telling you right now." There was a pause and then, "Longarm, *I* just shot our boss, Billy Vail."

Longarm froze with one leg in his pants and one leg

in the air. Off balance and not sure that he'd heard correctly, he stared and then blurted, "What did you just say to me?"

"I just shot Marshal Vail in the gut and now I'm going to do the same to you!"

With only one leg in his pants and with his gun resting on the bed, Longarm knew he had no chance at all of defending himself. He had been caught off guard and he was about to become a dead man. Buying a few precious seconds to gather his wits, he asked, "Why, Eli? Why in blazes would you shoot Marshal Vail? He's a good man and he's always been fair. He picked you out of a lot of other candidates for the job and that badge you're wearing."

The tall, hatchet-faced man wearing a drooping mustache laughed a bitter, ugly sound. "Billy Vail gave *you* the assignment I wanted in Arizona."

"You mean the shooting in Prescott?"

"Yes! The man shot was the territorial governor. And catching the shooter would have made me a big name. Would have earned me some respect up in our office."

"But . . ."

"Shut up and listen to me!" Pittman screamed. "I was a lawman in the Arizona Territory, so I'm the one that should have been assigned that job. But you . . . Billy's golden boy got it."

"It's your case," Longarm lied.

"Too late now. When Vail refused to change his mind and give me that assignment, I waited until tonight and then I slipped in through his back door after he and his wife went to sleep and I shot him in his gawdamn bed."

"Eli, you are a miserable, twisted son of a bitch!"

Longarm raged. "I had a bad feeling about you the moment we laid eyes upon each other."

"I never liked you, either. You, always getting the publicity. Always getting the prettiest women in town to fuss about you and then spread their legs for you. Too famous, Longarm. You were just too famous and now I'm going to become famous too."

"Your fame will last about as long as it takes you to drop through the trapdoor and dance at the end of a hangman's rope."

"We'll just see about that, Longarm. I've got a hunch that I'm going to get away with killing both of you."

"You know that's not going to happen."

"All I know is that putting a bullet in your belly is going to be something I'll enjoy," Pittman grated, the gun lifting slightly in his steady hand.

"Hold on!" Longarm said. "Maybe . . ."

"Shut up and die like a man!" Pittman chuckled.

"You've been drinking. Maybe I can get Mr. Vail to . . ."

"He's dead, you dumb bastard. I just told you I shot him in his damned bed."

"Billy is strong. Maybe he's going to make it."

"He *won't* make it. And the only reason you're still alive is that I wanted you to know who killed your friend and why," Eli Pittman snarled, cocking back the hammer of his gun. "If it's any consolation, I'm sure the town will give you and Billy one hell of a grand funeral."

Longarm was standing two feet in front of his second-story window, and that frosted pane of glass offered him the only chance he had at living, so he twisted and dived for the window just as the gun in Pittman's fist belched fire and lead.

Longarm felt the sharp glass cutting into his scalp and hands, and he also felt the impact of a slug against his body. He was falling and then striking the sloping porch and tumbling, only to fall again into the street below. Still conscious, he tried to drag himself upright by grabbing a hitching post. Deputy Marshal Pittman would most likely be coming to finish him off. At this time on a Sunday morning in downtown Denver the streets would be empty except for a few drunks passed out on the boardwalk. And maybe, because of the cold, even the drunks would have found shelter.

Gasping and feeling like his chest was collapsing, Longarm staggered onto the boardwalk and gazed wildly around looking for help. There wasn't a human in sight and here he was shot, cut to pieces from glass, probably broken in places that he didn't even realize because of the bad fall out of his window, and most importantly, he was unarmed.

Knowing he had only a minute or two left before Pittman busted outside into the street, Longarm lunged forward toward the thick trees that lined Cherry Creek. If he could reach them, he might be able to hide from Pittman long enough to figure out some way to survive until he could get help. Or maybe he'd just bleed to death beside the creek and his body would be found by someone taking their early morning Sunday stroll.

"Run!" he growled as he began to hobble faster toward the trees. "Run for your life!"

Behind him a door slammed shut and Pittman shouted,

"I see you headin' for the creek, Longarm! Stop and die like a man!"

Longarm did not want to die like a man. He wanted to run for his life and recover, then kill Eli Pittman. That was his goal, and even now as he reached the big cottonwood trees and his long legs slashed through the grass, he heard two more gunshots and swore that he could feel hot bullets whizzing past his head.

"I'm coming after you!"

Longarm was dodging through the cottonwoods, breath ragged in his mouth, lungs on fire, running like a cougar with hounds on his tail. He was scared, mad, and determined all at once.

Cherry Creek was not much more than a trickle at this time of year, and there was no chance of diving into it and being carried downstream. Longarm frantically looked for some place to hide. Some place where he could go to ground and that Pittman would not have time to search out. Staggering upstream in shallow water for fifty feet and feeling weaker with every unsteady step, he spied a big cottonwood that had been knocked down by a recent storm and a flood that had turned it facing the current. The huge tree had grown for years half-in and half-out of the stream, and now its black roots reminded Longarm of a witch's crooked fingers reaching up to grab the moon. Longarm thought he saw a muddy crater under those roots and he jumped for it. The water was shockingly cold and momentarily cleared his clotted mind. Knowing that Eli Pittman couldn't be far behind, Longarm began to burrow into the wet earth and cover himself with mud.

Had Pittman seen where he had gone to ground? Certainly he had left no tracks, because he had stayed in the shallow creek.

"Longarm! I'm going to kill you!"

Longarm pressed hard back under the roots and tried to slow his breathing even as waves of dizziness came and went. If Pittman caught him in this place, it would be a very bad ending. Longarm had never felt more helpless in his entire life, and now it was just a waiting game. Pittman wouldn't give up the search quickly or easily, but dawn was coming soon, and with it would be people.

"Hang on!" Longarm whispered to himself. "Hang on so the day will come when you can find and kill this murdering bastard for Billy Vail!"

Longarm bit his lower lip hard, tasting blood. He did not want to pass out in this hiding place. He was bleeding badly, and if he lost consciousness he would most likely die here like a damned, stinking muskrat.

And that was not the way any man ought to go.

Chapter 2

Longarm had drifted in and out of consciousness for hours, and it was mid-morning before he became sufficiently lucid and able to claw his way out of his hiding place, only to fall face-first into the cold creek. Because it was Sunday and because Cherry Creek had walking paths on both shores, he was immediately spotted and the strollers immediately rushed to his assistance.

"Easy! Easy!" a man kept shouting. "He's been shot in the side and someone has slashed him with a knife! Oh my god, he's dying!"

"Get a doctor! Someone find a doctor!" a woman cried.

Longarm knew that he wasn't going to die, but he also knew that he had been wounded and badly cut by his own shattered windowpane. He weakly splashed cold water to wash the mud off his face and clear his eyes. He was surprised to see that quite a Sunday crowd had already gathered.

"Someone get a lawman here! Maybe he's a killer!"

"I'm a lawman," Longarm mumbled. "But my badge is up in my apartment."

"Why, that's Deputy United States Marshal Custis Long! He's famous!"

"He's a mess," said a matronly woman with her nose up in the air. "And he's not even properly dressed. He's disgraceful!"

Longarm heard all this while in preparation to climb to his feet. He didn't know if his manhood was hanging out of his red flannel long johns or maybe he was bare-assed, and he really didn't care. All that mattered to him was to get patched up and see if Billy Vail was still fighting for his life at the downtown hospital.

Revenge against Eli would come later, just as surely as day followed dawn.

"Here," a man said, reaching down to give Longarm a helping hand, "let me help you to your feet."

"Is anything personal hanging out in the wind?"

"No. We'll get you a blanket. Your skin is almost blue with cold and you're covered with blood."

"Can you see where I was shot?" Longarm asked.

"No," the man said. "Too much mud and blood for that right now. But I would say that, if you were shot, it must not have been a killing wound."

"That stands to reason," Longarm agreed, allowing himself to be pulled upright while the crowd grew larger and some began to point and cover their faces.

"Actually, your most personal part *is* hanging out," the man whispered with embarrassment. "And I don't want to be the one to stuff it back into your long johns."

Despite the pain and circumstances, Longarm barked a laugh, reached down, and stuffed his manhood into his soggy underwear. "I hope there isn't a damned photographer on the way."

"If there is," the man said, "I'll block his view. You've really been through quite enough for today."

A woman of about thirty waded out into the creek with a gray wool blanket. "Here," she said, offering it to him. "You are cold and wet and badly hurt. I can see that you are almost ready to go into shock and we must get you to the hospital."

"Thank you, Miss . . ."

"Miss Danby," she said. "I'm a nurse at the hospital. I was on my way there this morning when you tumbled out from under those tree roots. At first I thought my eyes were deceiving me. You looked . . . Well, let's just say you looked like some horrible mud monster."

"The man who shot me is a rogue lawman," Longarm said. "He works for the United States Marshal's Office and his name is Deputy Marshal Eli Pittman and he must be escaping from Denver even as we're standing here talking. I need to speak to the sheriff or some deputy. Stone has to be captured before he gets away."

"Calm down," Miss Danby urged. "Let's get you to the hospital, and then we can see what can be done about this Marshal Eli Pittman."

"But he's getting away!" Longarm protested.

"Calm down, please," she insisted. "You have lost a lot of blood and you could go into shock and die. If that happens, will you be able to bring Marshal Pittman to justice?"

"No," Longarm admitted, "I suppose not."

"Then let's get you taken care of and then we'll worry about justice."

"The man that shot me also shot my boss, Marshal Vail. Do you know if . . ."

"I'm sorry," she told him. "I've been off for a few days and I was just about to go on my shift. But you shouldn't be worrying about anyone's health other than your own."

Longarm clamped his jaw shut and allowed them to help him out of the creek. The nurse called, "We need transportation. This man isn't strong enough to walk to the hospital."

"Here comes a buggy!"

"Then stop him and ask him if he will please help us get this fine marshal to the hospital. Tell him I'll pay him for his trouble."

"You're very kind," Longarm told the woman. "But I could have walked just the short distance."

"In your soggy red flannel underwear?" She shook her pretty head. "Don't be ridiculous, Marshal Long."

Longarm guessed that would look pretty ridiculous. And as they helped him into the hastily summoned buggy, he collapsed on the seat cushions and heard Miss Danby shout, "To the hospital just as fast as you can!"

The door slammed shut and Longarm closed his eyes. Miss Danby was obviously a person who knew how to take charge of things in an emergency. He was grateful to her for that, but about all that he could think of was getting to Billy Vail's bedside and making a vow that he would hunt down Eli Pittman if it was the last thing he ever did in this life.

Chapter 3

"Is Billy Vail still alive?" Longarm asked the moment they arrived at the hospital. "He's my boss and best friend."

"I can't tell you that," a doctor said, rushing to his side and lifting the blanket to study Longarm's bullet wound. "Marshal Vail is in the operating room, and I can only say that the surgeon is doing everything he can to save the man's life. From what I've heard from the staff, I'm afraid that Marshal Vail's chances are slim."

Longarm clenched both fists at his sides. "If Billy pulls through, I need to talk to him right away."

"Let's see if we can get you taken care of and then we'll worry about Marshal Vail."

The young doctor ordered a nurse to clean Longarm's side, and then he bent and carefully probed the bullet wound with his forceps. "Looks like you got very lucky. The bullet appears to have cracked your rib and then ricocheted off it. It left a glancing bullet wound with clear entry and exit point holes. The wound is contaminated, but it's not leaking much blood. The main thing we all have to worry about at this point is an infection."

"If you clean it up and throw some medicinal salve on it, I'll be fine," Longarm assured the doctor.

"I expect that's true, but that cracked rib is going to give you a great deal of pain."

"I can handle the pain. How deep are the wounds that I got when I dived through my upstairs window?"

The doctor glanced at his face then gently probed his scalp. "The deepest cut you have is over your right ear. That one will probably need stitching. The other wounds are superficial. You must have protected your face with your forearm and that's why it's also lacerated."

"I acted purely on instinct," Longarm confessed. "I got caught flat-footed and there was only one way to escape and that was through the window."

"You're fortunate that the fall didn't break your neck or at least some bones."

Longarm nodded. "Yeah, I got very lucky. I thought he was going to run me down and kill me along Cherry Creek."

"I understand that a fellow officer of the law shot Marshal Vail as well as yourself."

"That's right. I never liked the man and he snapped. I'll go after him and make sure that he never carries a badge or tries to kill someone by surprise again."

"One bad apple ruins the barrel," the doctor said. "You can bet that there will be a lot of front page publicity about this."

"I don't read the newspaper articles when they talk about crime and law officers," Longarm admitted. "But I'm sure that you're right. On another subject, what happened to Miss Danby? She was here just a minute ago."

"Nurse Danby went to assist the surgeon that is trying to save your boss's life. She's the best that we have when it comes to emergencies in our operating room."

Longarm thought back to how she had taken charge down at Cherry Creek. "She's quite a woman, all right."

The doctor turned and gave Longarm a hard look. "Yes, she is the kind of woman you would like to have standing by your side if you were in trouble . . . any kind of trouble at all."

Longarm grinned and nodded his head in agreement. "Not to mention that Miss Danby is sure easy on the eyes."

The surgeon, who was younger than Longarm and quite handsome, raised his eyebrows. "Let me see if I've got this right. Your boss is fighting for his life and you've lost way too much blood and now you're telling me that you find Miss Danby *attractive*?"

Longarm shrugged, not sure what was needling the doctor. "It was just an idle observation, Doctor. I certainly didn't mean any disrespect toward Nurse Danby. I did, however, want to express my appreciation for the way that she handled herself and the other people down on Cherry Creek when they found me about half-frozen in that water."

"I'm sure she doesn't need your praise, Marshal Long. And while we are talking about Miss Danby, I have to say that I've heard about your reputation as a skirt chaser and it appears that it is well deserved."

"Are you a minister or an ordained preacher every Sunday? Is that what this is about?" Longarm asked, starting to get annoyed.

"No. Just a doctor."

"Then you ought to stick to medicine." When the doctor flushed with anger, Longarm added, "Why don't we admit that for some reason we don't like each other? And then you can get on with stitching up my scalp and I can lie down a few minutes and rest."

"That's a good idea," the doctor said, "but you should know that Miss Danby is not only the best nurse in this hospital, but she's *my* girl."

Longarm had to smile. Here he was all beat up, covered with mud and cut to pieces, and this man was jealous of him. "Congratulations, Doc. You'd make a very striking couple."

"I think so," the young doctor said, threading a suture through a curved needle. "And one of these days you'll read our wedding announcement in the newspaper. My name, so you'll know it when you read it, is Dr. Robert Gaylord."

Longarm pretended to be impressed. "Dr. Robert Gaylord, huh? Would you be related to . . ."

"Yes," the doctor interrupted as he knotted the suture and began to clip away a patch of Longarm's hair. "Senator Gaylord is my father."

"Well how about that!" Longarm exclaimed. "No wonder Miss Danby agreed to marry you. Why, you not only have an esteemed profession, but you have family money and family power. You are *indeed* a privileged man, Dr. Gaylord!"

"I consider myself blessed that Miss Danby has seen fit to honor me with her affections."

"Are you *formally* engaged?"

The doctor blinked and then frowned. "And exactly why do you ask?"

"Because I didn't notice an engagement ring on Miss Danby's finger. Just curious, I guess. Curiosity comes with my profession."

Gaylord blustered. "We haven't been formally engaged, but she'll soon be wearing my ring. I've already bought and paid for it. A full carat."

"How impressive."

"Yes, isn't it," the doctor said as he suddenly and without warning dug the curved needle into Longarm's scalp.

"Ouch! Take it easy, dammit!"

"Hurt, does it?"

"Yeah, as a matter of fact."

"I thought all of you marshals were big and tough."

Longarm had had just about enough of this edgy banter. "Doc," he said, "you say that I've lost a lot of blood, cracked a rib, and am in sorry physical shape. But if we went out into a back alley, I'd be all over you like a bird on a bug."

The doctor flushed with anger. "Marshal, unlike yourself, I'm not a back alley fighter, but I've been a student of the manly art of boxing and I can handle myself quite well in the ring."

"That may be true, Doc, but if you fought me, you'd find out that I don't fight fair. I fight to win."

"I'm sure that you do. But just remember that I'm rich and successful and you're nothing but a low-paid marshal who will probably end up in a cheap pine coffin with an unmarked grave."

Longarm had a powerful urge to smack this arrogant asshole alongside the head, but he held himself in check. "I just want Billy Vail to pull through."

"We're doing all that we can to make that happen," Dr. Gaylord snapped. "But as for yourself, you're going to need to stay in this hospital tonight."

"So you can order a nurse to administer poison?"

Dr. Gaylord shook his head as if Longarm was hopeless. "Not funny, Marshal. Not at all funny. I'm a healer. You're the killer working behind a badge."

"I guess you could look at it that way," Longarm said. "Until someone put your life in danger or beat hell out of you and you howled for justice. If that happened, I think you might have an entirely different point of view about what my role as a lawman really is."

"I've got more important things to do than to banter with you," the doctor told him. "Just follow my orders until you are discharged from this hospital and we won't cross swords."

For a moment, Longarm considered telling this high-and-mighty doctor that he would come and go as he pleased. But then he realized that he couldn't stay much closer to his boss than he was right now. "I'll stay overnight, Doc. Just keep me informed about Marshal Vail."

"I'll have the nurses keep you informed. I've got far more important things to do while I'm on duty."

"Sure you do," Longarm growled.

Longarm must have been given a sedative to put him to sleep, and when he awoke, it was dark outside his private room and there was an attractive young nurse at his bedside balancing a tray, soap, and a washbasin. She was smiling, and when Longarm followed her glance he saw that she had pulled off the sheet he'd been lying under and was admiring his naked body.

"Nurse, I expect that you see naked men all the time. What is so interesting about my scarred and battered carcass?"

"Dr. Gaylord ordered me to give you a bed bath. You're a muddy mess, Marshal."

"A bed bath?"

"Sure. I'm good at them. You'll like it and you won't even have to put your feet on the floor."

"Sounds interesting if the circumstances were different," Longarm drawled. "But I'd rather climb into a bathtub under my own power, if it is all the same to you and the good doctor."

"Oh, but you'll *love* my bed baths!" She winked. "And it isn't every day that I get to bathe a handsome and famous lawman."

"Sounds like a lot of unnecessary bother."

"No bother at all. My name is Betty. Miss Betty Horner and I enjoy giving bed baths ... most of the time." She set the basin and soap down on a little bedside table and ran her fingers lightly across his thighs. "The only thing you need to do is just close your eyes and enjoy the experience."

Her fingers gently moved up to caress his manhood. "I promise that you're going to really like this. So relax."

Longarm shrugged his broad shoulders, and as Betty's soft fingers played with his privates, he decided he wouldn't mind a bed bath so much after all.

Chapter 4

Longarm lay stretched out on the hospital bed with his eyes closed just enjoying the experience. He was not in the habit of having a pretty nurse bathe him with warm, scented water, and he thought a man could get quite accustomed to this very pleasurable experience.

"Roll over on your other side so I can wash that part of your back," she ordered.

Longarm obliged. He happened to look down, and damned if his big stiffy wasn't a dead giveaway to his rising desire.

"Been a nurse for very long?" he asked, trying to turn his mind from the thoughts he was having.

"About three years. How does this feel on your back?"

"Pure heaven," he confessed.

"You sure have a lot of scars, Marshal Long."

"I've been attacked more times than I care to admit."

"Roll back onto your back while I do your . . . My goodness!" she said with a giggle as she stroked his hard shaft. "I'd say you're *really* enjoying this bed bath!"

He felt his cheeks burn with embarrassment. "Nurse," he said in a thick voice. "I know that you're just following the doctor's orders, but I doubt what you're doin' was ordered by the doctor."

"Don't be too sure of that."

"Meanin'?"

"Well, Dr. Gaylord is pretty jealous about his intended and he wanted to make sure that you were well taken care of tonight."

Longarm suddenly pushed himself up on his elbows. "Are you sayin' that Gaylord ordered you to . . . well, do what you're doin' to me?"

"No," she said, leaning over and blowing hot breath on his stiff manhood. "But the doctor is a very jealous man and he thinks you needed some extra attention tonight."

Longarm clucked his tongue in amazement. "I don't understand what is going on here, but I'm likin' it a lot. How far are you prepared to go with this, Betty? Because if you're just gonna breathe on my little man, then I think we had better put a stop to this. But . . ."

Her head dipped and her mouth enveloped his manhood. It was so warm, and sudden, that it almost took Longarm's breath away. He stroked the nurse's wavy brown hair and said, "I guess you just answered my question. You're prepared to go all the way."

She looked up and gave him a wet smile. "Didn't you figure that out when I came into your room and locked the door from the inside?"

"I wasn't payin' much attention to my door at the time."

"Well pay attention now, Marshal, because I'm going

to show you what an *experienced* nurse can really do for a favored patient!"

Longarm grinned from ear to ear as Betty undressed and then climbed over the top of him.

"Easy on the cracked rib," he whispered. "It's a little ouchy."

"It's not the cracked rib that interests me," she said, wiggling her round bottom downward like a hen lowering itself on a nest of eggs. "But I'll try not to be too rough."

"You are a kind, kind woman," Longarm groaned. "A credit to your profession."

"Shut up and get to work," she laughed, dropping her melon breasts into his face and wiggling them so that they tickled his nose and lips.

Longarm hadn't thought that he was up to this kind of pleasuring tonight. And it was damned shameful to be enjoying himself so much when Billy Vail was somewhere nearby fighting for his life. But he knew Billy would have told him to take advantage of the gift and enjoy it as long as it was hot and ready.

So Longarm growled low in his throat, inhaled a full mouthful of one fleshy melon and gave everything he had into sweet Nurse Betty.

When she dressed and prepared to leave his little hospital room, Longarm felt like he was floating on a cloud. "Can you get Dr. Gaylord to authorize my staying another night?"

She giggled. "I might be able to do that."

"I hope you can," Longarm said. "What time are you going off shift?"

"At seven in the morning."

"Well," he said with a laugh in his voice, "I wouldn't mind being awakened and given some . . . um . . . special healing."

"I'll definitely see what I can do."

"Betty? If you could find out how Billy Vail is doing, I'd sure appreciate it."

"He means a lot to you."

"Yeah," Longarm said, "he does. If Billy doesn't make it, I'll be on the killer's trail tomorrow, and I won't stop until I find him."

"And if your boss does survive?"

"I'll wait a day just to make sure my boss is on his way to a full recovery, and then I'll go after the man that did this."

"You saw him?"

"Oh, yeah! I saw him and he saw me. And I'm sure he knows that I won't stop until I kill him or see him hanged."

"I understand and I'll be right back with whatever news I can find out about Mr. Vail."

"Thank you," Longarm said.

"You're welcome. It won't be long."

The door shut, and Longarm thought about his boss fighting for his life maybe even in the adjoining room. Billy was a good man. Really the best. Longarm wasn't sure that he would even want to remain a federal officer of the law if Billy Vail died.

Ten minutes later, Nurse Betty slipped back into Longarm's room. "I have good news!"

"He's going to make it?"

"Definitely. The surgeon removed the slugs and your boss is going to pull through, although it will take weeks, maybe even months before he is able to leave this hospital."

"Billy is a fighter. I'm betting he'll be out of here in a week and back at his home."

She shrugged. "So this means that you still want me to ask Dr. Gaylord if you can stay one more night?"

Longarm nodded. "As long as you're willing to give me another bed bath and . . . you know."

"I know, and I'm not only willing, I'm eager and ready," she said, winking at him from the door. "Now get some sleep. You've lost a lot of blood and you need your rest."

"I can rest tomorrow," he said. "But if I get another chance at you before daylight, Betty, you know I'm going to make the most of it."

"Me too," she giggled. "But right now I've got other patients that need attention."

She shut the door and Longarm laced his hands behind his head. He didn't know much about life and especially about women, but if he were a betting man, he'd bet that Nurse Betty was going to come back well before daybreak.

Chapter 5

Longarm stood at Billy Vail's bedside and looked down at his friend and boss. And although Longarm wouldn't have said it out loud, Billy looked to have aged about ten years since he'd been shot and nearly killed by a man he had trusted enough to hire as a federal law officer.

"Why are you staring at me that way?" Billy asked, his voice weak.

"What way?"

"As if I'm Lazarus raised from the dead?"

"You damn near died, Billy. The surgeon said that most men would have died given the bullets you took from Eli Pittman."

"I have been thinking about Pittman, and the more I think the more confused I become. I have no earthly idea why he shot me. I guess something deep inside of him just snapped and I happened to be in the wrong place at the wrong time."

"There was more to it than that, Billy. Pittman was furious that he didn't get the Arizona assignment."

"And *that*'s why he shot me and tried to kill you?"

"That's right."

Billy Vail shook his head in amazement. "I hired Pittman. I knew that he had some problems in his past, but I thought he was going to make a fine United States marshal."

"We can't be right all the time. I never liked the man from the first day that I laid eyes upon him."

"Is that a fact?"

"It is," Longarm said. "There was just something about him . . . in his eyes maybe . . . that told me he wasn't quite right in the head."

"Well I sure wish you'd have told me that before this all happened."

"I did try to tell you," Longarm replied. "You've just forgotten my warning."

"He's got to be caught and put behind bars as fast as we can find him. I know that the newspapers are going to be clamoring for answers about why a deputy marshal damn near killed us."

"The hell with the newspapers," Longarm said. "The newspapers are always looking to rake up dirt and make everything overblown. I have yet to see an honest article when it comes to law enforcement officers."

"I definitely share that attitude, but a rogue lawman is always big news."

Wanting to change the subject, Longarm said, "I'm sure that Pittman has left Denver by now."

"And where do you think he has gone?"

"He's gone to Arizona. As you will remember, Pittman was from the Arizona Territory. I'm sure that he had a lot of friends who would have been mighty impressed had he gotten the assignment and made the arrest."

"I suppose so."

"And," Longarm continued, "I wouldn't be surprised if, in his mind, he'd conjured up images of being feted as a big hero. Maybe he had a woman there that had spurned him and he was trying to win her back and impress her. Maybe there were other people he wanted to impress or he had his eyes on some plum job in Arizona."

"You're coming up with a lot of maybes," Billy said.

"All right, can you think of any other reason why getting that Arizona assignment was so important that . . . when you gave it to me instead of him . . . he suddenly went kill-crazy?"

"No, I can't."

"The reasons don't matter," Longarm said. "All that really matters is that I track him down and bring him back for justice."

"Since it appears that I'm going to pull through this, and you don't seem too much the worse for wear, then I expect a judge and jury won't sentence him to be hanged."

"Probably not," Longarm agreed. "But you can be pretty damn sure that he will spend a lot of years in prison."

"Pittman won't surrender peaceably," Billy mused. "I'm convinced that he'll go down fighting."

"I'm counting on that."

Billy's eyebrows knitted in worry. "I've seen him handle a revolver, and he's pretty impressive."

"Did you see him draw and fire?"

"Just draw. He was showing off, which I didn't appreciate, but when he did some gun tricks and I saw how fast he was, I couldn't help but think that I'd never seen any man handle a Colt better."

"So you're trying to tell me not to face him and demand that he surrender because, if it comes down to a draw and shoot . . . I'll lose?"

Billy cast his eyes around the room for a moment. "Longarm, I know that you're fast, and much more important, you're accurate and cool under fire. But I'm telling you that Eli Pittman has the fastest draw that I've ever seen and if you were facing him, he would have his gun out first and kill you."

"That's always a good thing to know," Longarm said, not a bit impressed. "I'll just have to get the drop on the treacherous son of a bitch."

"Yeah," Billy said, "that's what you'll have to do if you want to live long enough to inherit my job and desk."

"I don't want either your desk or your paperwork job," Longarm told his boss. "But I would like to grow fat and lazy like you."

Billy grinned. "You big bastard! I could fire you for insulting me like that."

"You could, but you won't."

"So when are you leaving for Arizona?"

"Tomorrow," Longarm told the man.

"Why not today? You look like you could stand up to the train trip."

"The doctor wants me to stay another night just to make sure that I'm up to snuff. I did lose quite a bit of blood."

"Then you *should* remain here at the hospital one more night." Billy studied Longarm silently for a moment. "But you're not the kind of man to linger an extra twenty-four hours just to regenerate some lost blood. So what is the real reason you aren't on your way to the train station?"

Longarm grinned. "Dammit, Billy, I never could put anything over on you."

"Nope, and I've never understood why you still try."

"It's a . . ."

"Woman," Billy said with certainty. "You've found a woman and you want to bed her one more night before you leave for Arizona."

"That's about the size of it."

"Who is she? If I may be so bold as to ask."

"A nurse."

Billy's jaw dropped. "You're humpin' one of our nurses?"

"She started it all off by giving me a bed bath."

"A bed bath?"

"Yep. And she decided to do me a little extra."

"Well I might want her to give *me* a bed bath!"

"You're a married man with children . . . all of whom have been at your bedside since you arrived. I don't think you want the kind of bed bath that I received."

"Yeah," Billy finally agreed. "I guess that wouldn't go over too well with the little woman."

"Not at all well."

"Still," Billy said, giving him a sly wink, "you have definitely piqued my curiosity."

"Then let's keep it 'piqued,'" Longarm said.

"Turd!"

"It's for your own good," Longarm told the man. "I just don't want you to be tempted into sin. And besides that, I really like your wife."

"Aw, hell, you're right. But dammit, I can't help but wonder which nurse you're ballin' and how it would feel to get a special bed bath."

Longarm patted his friend's arm. "Maybe someday I'll tell you all about it, but not now."

"Why not?"

"Don't want to get your blood pressure to go way up," Longarm answered as he left the man's room.

Longarm was dozing in his hospital bed when his door was pushed open. His first thought and hope was that Nurse Betty had come for a preview of the night's pleasures, but instead it was Nurse Danby.

"I just came on shift and I wanted to check in and see how you are doing," she said, holding a metal chart in her hands. "It says that you are well on your way to a full and speedy recovery."

Longarm had forgotten just how attractive Nurse Danby was, which was not surprising considering how and where they had first met. "I'll be discharged tomorrow morning."

"Dr. Gaylord wanted you to stay an extra day just to make sure that you are well on your way to a full recovery."

"Yeah, he was real concerned about me," Longarm said, trying to keep the sarcasm out of his voice. "I understand that you and Dr. Gaylord are soon going to be engaged."

Her smile melted and she came into the room, closing

the door behind her. "Is that what Robert . . . I mean Dr. Gaylord told you?"

"Yep. Are you surprised? Have I misspoke?"

She looked distressed. "I . . . I'm just a bit taken aback. Dr. Gaylord is a fine man and doctor, but he's a little presumptuous."

"So you're *not* going to marry him?"

"I haven't actually decided, although I've no idea why we are discussing a matter that is so very personal."

"I'm sorry," Longarm said, "but I was just making pleasant conversation and I had no idea that it might upset you."

"Did Dr. Gaylord say anything else about me?"

"I'm afraid that I should just keep my mouth shut and not risk upsetting you again."

She came right up to his bed with a very serious expression on her pretty face. "Marshal, I need to know."

Longarm frowned. "All right. He said that he had already bought you an engagement ring and it was a full carat."

Her eyes widened in surprise. "Robert said that?"

"He did. A carat is pretty impressive. You ought to be squealing with joy."

"I don't 'squeal' under any circumstances," the nurse said with annoyance. "And I find it very unsettling that he is telling anyone . . . especially a patient . . . that we are going to become engaged."

"I'd think he would be quite the catch. He told me who his father is, and that means that Dr. Gaylord is both rich and well connected. And I suppose most women would think that he is handsome. So what is the problem, Nurse Danby?"

"The problem is that no woman wants to be taken for granted! That's what the problem is, Marshal Long. Sure, Dr. Gaylord seems to be a wonderful catch, but he can be cold, distant, and even exasperatingly arrogant."

"I find that impossible to believe," Longarm lied.

"It's true. He comes from a very privileged background, and I think he thinks just a little too much of himself at times."

"Actually," Longarm admitted, enjoying this conversation immensely, "I kind of had the same impression."

"Well there we are then," Nurse Danby said with a curt nod of her chin. "And I'm not saying that I will *never* marry the man. I'm only saying that I haven't decided and I won't be pushed into making such an important and lifelong decision."

"That sounds like the most reasonable attitude to take."

"Are you humoring me?" she asked, leaning over his bed. "Is that what you are doing?"

"Heck no!" Longarm protested. "I was just trying to be agreeable."

She folded her arms across her chest. "Your face is all cut up, but none of the lacerations are deep. When I first saw you standing in Cherry Creek you were almost ready to go into shock, and I'm sure you are aware that shock can be and often is fatal."

"I thank you for your help," he said sincerely. "You were amazingly calm under the circumstances."

The compliment caused her to relax. "It's because that is how I've been trained to react in a medical emergency."

"I'm sure that's it."

The nurse studied him for a moment, and then she

said, "I'm going to take a look at your dressings and see how you are coming along. Won't take but a minute."

"I'm in no hurry," he told her. "What part of my body are you most interested in seeing?"

She shook her head, but he could tell that she was fighting off a smile. "You are quite the character, Marshal. I've heard of you, and I have the impression that you are intent on living up to your rather unsavory reputation."

"'Unsavory'?" he repeated. "My goodness, Nurse Danby. I do believe that I've been insulted. I might begin to sulk and pout."

"No you won't," she said, peeling back the sheet that covered him and then gently removing the bandages over his ribs. "You won't feel insulted because your ego is too bedrock solid."

"How's it look?" he asked, studying the wound that she had revealed in his side.

"It looks clean and there is no sign of infection."

"That's great."

"I'll replace the bandages. But first, I want to take a look at that nasty scalp wound."

She bent forward, and he could smell the sweet scent of roses. Her full breasts strained at her nurse's uniform, and it was all that Longarm could do to behave himself.

"Did Dr. Gaylord really put in those stitches?" she asked with concern and a look of disapproval.

"Yep. Why do you ask?"

"He usually does a much neater job."

"Well," Longarm explained, "I might have annoyed him a bit just before he started the stitching."

"And how did you do that?"

"I told him that I thought you were very easy on the eyes."

She stepped back quickly. "You said that about me?"

"I did and it's the truth. And now I know that you smell like roses and you have a very nice and well-rounded body."

"Marshal Long!" she protested. "I won't be talked to in that manner!"

He tried to look at least slightly contrite. "Please accept my apology for saying what is obviously the truth."

"You are *really* impossible!"

"I have been called much worse."

"I'm going to go and get some fresh bandaging, and I want you to just lie still and reflect on how a gentleman should converse with a lady."

"I'm not a gentleman anymore," he confessed. "I was once . . . but that was quite a few years ago when I was raised in West Virginia. And to be honest, Nurse Danby, I don't think of you as a lady but as my rescuer and a professional nurse."

"Oh really?" she asked, raising her eyebrows in what he thought might be amusement.

"That's right. I'm the patient and you're the nurse, and I'm a man and you're a very stimulating woman."

She clucked her tongue. "I think I'm going to see if Nurse Horner will take care of you and do your bandaging. I simply do not have the patience for someone so . . . so insolent."

"Nurse Betty Horner would be happy to take care of me, but I think that she is waiting to do that tonight."

Nurse Danby's eyes widened. "Don't you dare be

insinuating that Nurse Horner is anything but a professional!"

"Oh, she's a professional all right. Gives amazing bed baths. I've got no complaints about Nurse Betty Horner, and in fact, I think you should ask her to change my bandages. I'd no doubt find it a lot more pleasant than if you do the job."

The flush of her skin told Longarm that he'd wounded her professional pride. "I'll do the bandaging. I'd not trust poor Nurse Horner to be safe in this room alone with a predator like you."

"Always looking out for someone else," he said. "Just like you've been taught by your elders and superiors."

"You are the most . . . the most irritating patient I think that I've ever known!"

"And you," Longarm said, "are probably the sweetest-smelling nurse I've ever known. I'm leaving tomorrow for the Arizona Territory, but I'll remember the scent of you, Nurse Danby."

"You're going after the marshal who shot you and Mr. Vail." It was not a question, but rather a statement of fact.

"I am."

"You really should rest at your apartment for a few days. You lost quite a lot of blood."

"I'll be all right. I'll have my own little sleeping compartment and I'll do nothing but rest all the way to Flagstaff."

"I have heard of Arizona since I was a young girl. Isn't it all desert country?"

"No. A lot of the northern and eastern part of the territory is mountainous. But there are parts of the territory that are blistering hot in the summertime. As hot as hell, I'd expect."

She smiled. "Oh, I doubt that."

"I've been in Yuma a few times. Once in the summer when I was on a manhunt. I nearly died of the heat. The fugitive I was after did die of heatstroke. Down in the low desert, a man won't last long without a lot of water."

"I wouldn't like the desert. Are the mountains of Arizona like our Colorado Mountains?"

"Sort of. Not as big or as tall. But they're nice. And near where I'm bound is the Grand Canyon."

"Is it as magnificent as they say?"

"Even more so."

"I'd give anything to see it someday."

"Why wait?" he said without thinking. "Why not go to see it with me?"

She laughed. "Are you insane?"

"No. I'm attracted to you and I do owe you an immense favor."

"You don't owe me anything, Marshal Long."

"I disagree and I'll be leaving tomorrow at ten o'clock. Having you as a traveling companion would be wonderful."

She threw up her hands in exasperation. "Marshal, you are way beyond incorrigible!"

"Glad you think so."

He had flustered her beyond his expectations, and when Nurse Danby stormed out of his room all stiff-backed to get bandaging, Longarm burst out laughing.

Chapter 6

Longarm left the hospital early that morning, and he was grateful to be discharged, because Nurse Betty had given him very little time to rest. He was exhausted and badly in need of sleep from the second night in a row of almost marathon lovemaking. But he had no time to think of sleep, because he had to go by the Federal Building and pick up some travel money as well as offer his fellow officers and workers an assurance that Billy Vail was on the road to recovery and eventually would be back at his desk.

"When we heard it was Eli Pittman who shot Marshal Vail and then you, we just couldn't believe it," one of the deputies said, echoing the thoughts of everyone in the office that morning. "What on earth could have gone so wrong with the man that he'd do such a terrible thing?"

"I don't know," Longarm said. "But the main thing is that Marshal Vail is going to be fine. It might take a while for him to fully regain his health, but it will happen."

"We all want to go after Pittman," one of the deputies said. "We're just itching to catch that bastard."

"I'm sure that Pittman is on his way to Arizona," Longarm told the collection of federal officers and office workers. "The thing that triggered his anger was that he didn't get the assignment. Pittman hailed from Arizona and felt that the assignment was his due. He probably had some pretty ambitious plans, and catching whoever shot and wounded the territorial governor was the springboard that he'd counted on."

"We would all like to go after him," a young marshal said.

"I know that, but there are other things to do here, and I'm the one that Pittman hates most. I let him get the drop on me at my apartment and I'm going to get some payback."

"So you're going to Arizona?"

"That's right," Longarm told them. "Marshal Vail gave me the Arizona assignment, and I'm going to add taking Pittman on as my reward."

"Kill him or bring him back so we can watch him face a long prison sentence," a clerk said angrily.

"That's my full intention," Longarm told them. "Now you all need to go about your jobs and keep your spirits up. I'm sure Marshal Vail will be sent home in a few days, and I'm equally sure that he'd enjoy some of you as visitors. Just don't all come on the same day, and be careful not to tax him too much. He was in bad shape and he'll need plenty of rest."

"You sure don't look too good yourself, Custis," one of the deputy marshals said. "In fact, you look terrible."

"I know. But I'll get some rest and recuperation on the train out to Arizona. In a week or two I'll be fine."

They nodded and then Longarm went about getting some money for his manhunt.

Afterward, he headed directly for his apartment to grab a satchel, some clothes, and various other personal items he would take to Arizona.

"I need to speak with you, Marshal Long!"

Longarm turned and saw his old battle-axe of a landlady coming in his direction just as he was locking his door to leave.

"Dammit!" he muttered under his breath, because he did not like Mrs. Henderson and she clearly did not approve of him. Longarm had lived in this apartment for almost a year and he had gotten into several arguments with Mrs. Henderson. She was in her sixties, prying, fat, and crotchety. He knew that one day he would blow his stack and then move to another apartment. But he liked the location of this one and the rent was cheap. Still and all, a man could only take so much harassment and then he had to speak his mind and face the consequences.

"Marshal, exactly who is going to pay for that window that you broke upstairs?"

"I really hadn't given it a thought," he said.

She planted her feet solidly on the floor. "Well, you'd *better* give it a thought. I won't have the weather let inside to ruin the floors and walls."

"I see your point, Mrs. Henderson. The window needs to be repaired immediately."

"All right then," she grumped. "At least you're responsible enough to understand that much. The window will probably cost about ten dollars to replace and since it is obvious that you are leaving for who knows where, I need that ten dollars right now."

"Why don't you just add it to my rent, which isn't due for another two weeks, Mrs. Henderson. I don't have time to go to the bank and get you the repair money this morning. I have a train to catch."

He tried to step around her, but Mrs. Henderson was a wide woman and she was quick enough to block his path. She stuck out her fat hand, palm up, and said, "Ten dollars or I'll toss your belongings in the hallway and you can consider yourself evicted."

"What?"

"You heard me. I don't like troublemakers living in my apartment, and I like even less that you seem to have a different woman every week coming up there for whatever unspeakable acts you perform."

"Now, wait just a darn minute, Mrs. Henderson," he sputtered. "I think you are completely exaggerating and being unreasonable."

"No I'm not! Or have you forgotten that my apartment is directly below yours and I have to endure listening to the moans and groans, squeals and hollerin' that go on in your apartment. My gawd, sometimes I think that you must be using whips and other vile devices on the women that are lured into your bed!"

"That's it!" Longarm growled. "I've had it with you, Mrs. Henderson. You're just a bored, nosey old hag who probably never once had a man make you scream with pleasure and delight."

Mrs. Henderson paled, and then she took a swing at Longarm, who easily ducked out of her range.

"You had better be out of here at the end of your two weeks or you'll find your things have been tossed into the alley!"

"I'm paid up for two more weeks," he said, biting out the words. "And if you even step foot in my apartment while I'm gone, I'll arrest you for trespassing and unlawful entry."

"What?"

"You heard me, you self-righteous old biddy! I'll arrest you and have you thrown in jail!"

Mrs. Henderson shook like a bowl of custard pudding. She was so mad that she was incapable of speech and merely hissed and sputtered. Longarm knew that he'd put fear into her, and he smiled. "I will have you thrown into a filthy jail cell, Mrs. Henderson."

Her hand flew to her mouth.

Longarm had taken so much grief from the woman that he pressed his advantage. "I'll have you thrown into a cell with a dirty mattress on the floor and hundreds of cockroaches crawling all over you."

"Oh my gawd!" she moaned. "No!"

"I'll do it if you ever give me another bad time about my guests or behavior. And that's a promise."

Mrs. Henderson slumped against the wall trembling.

Longarm expelled a deep breath and pointed a finger at her. "Mrs. Henderson, you may add ten dollars to my next month's rent and have the damned window fixed right away."

She managed to nod as Longarm hurried past on his way to the train depot. As he made his way down the street, he felt bad that he'd had to be so threatening. But Mrs. Henderson had been a thorn in his side for way too long, and now he'd finally managed to get the upper hand. He had a feeling that she would leave him alone from now on no matter how many and how often he brought women to his apartment.

At the Denver and Rio Grande train station Longarm bought a ticket and was about to climb aboard when he heard his name being called in a loud, shrill voice.

"Must be one of your women coming to bid you a fond farewell," the station attendant said. "She's a pretty one, too."

Longarm did a double take when he recognized Nurse Danby flying down the train platform toward him, and right behind her was Dr. Gaylord.

"Oh my gawd," he whispered, "Billy Vail must have suddenly died!"

Longarm braced himself for this terrible news, but to his amazement he saw Dr. Gaylord grab Nurse Danby, spin her around, and slap her across the face with the back of his hand.

Longarm dropped his bag and lurched forward, not sure what the hell was happening.

"Let me go!" she cried. "Leave me alone!"

"Damn you!" the doctor shouted. "You can't do this to me!"

"I'm finished with you!" she cried. "Now let me go!"

Longarm was running when he saw the arrogant doctor raise his hand and strike the nurse again, knocking her to the hard wooden platform.

Three strides more sent him crashing into the doctor, and they went down fighting.

Longarm was weak from his blood loss, but he was also furious, and his anger at seeing a woman mistreated goaded him into a frenzy. He and Gaylord were about the same size, but the doctor had not recently lost a few pints of precious blood. Even so, Longarm was the more experienced and stronger of the two, and he managed to get on top of the man and bash his handsome face three times with his fists.

Dr. Gaylord's nose splattered like a plate of spaghetti and his blood gushed. He howled, and Longarm grabbed his ears and smashed his head up and down on the wooden floor, again and again, until he felt people pulling him off the beaten and badly injured physician.

"Enough!" Nurse Danby was crying. "If you don't stop, you're going to kill Robert!"

"He deserves all the punishment I can serve out," Longarm growled, allowing himself to be pulled upright. "What the hell happened? Why did he hit you like that?"

"He was jealous of you."

"Me?"

"Yes, and when I refused to wear his engagement ring, Robert went insane with anger. I knew at that moment that I had to get away from him."

Longarm bit a hunk of skin off a badly skinned knuckle. "Why didn't you go to the local marshal's office and demand protection?"

"From a *Gaylord*? In *this* town?"

"I see your point," Longarm conceded. "So what are you going to do now?"

She lifted her chin in defiance and glared down at Dr. Gaylord for an instant. Then she turned her face up to Longarm and said, "I'm going to Arizona to see the Grand Canyon."

Longarm blinked with surprise, and then he heard the train attendant shout, "All aboard!"

"We'd better get on board," he told the nurse. "No sense in both of us missing this train."

"But I haven't even had time to buy a ticket yet."

"We'll do that after the train leaves," he told her. "Let's go!"

And so they jumped onto the train as it was leaving the station. They took a seat and watched as Dr. Robert Gaylord was finally helped to his feet with his face covered in blood.

"I don't understand why he would be jealous of me," Longarm said, "with cuts on my face and nothing to offer a woman in terms of stability; I'm no competition to a rich doctor."

"He thought you were."

"Then maybe Dr. Gaylord wasn't half as bright as he thought he was," Longarm said as the train picked up speed heading south out of Denver.

Chapter 7

Longarm sat relaxing in the Santa Fe's dining car, smoking a cigar and enjoying a glass of French brandy while admiring a stunning sunset splashing across New Mexico. He had slept very well in his private car the past three nights and was feeling almost up to snuff.

"Hello, Marshal," Nurse Danby said. "Enjoying the view?"

"I am! Would you care to join me?"

"I'd like that," she said.

"I'm drinking brandy . . . Would you care for some?"

"I'm not sure if I've ever had it. Does it taste like wine?"

"A bit stronger, I'd say. But it's not harsh like most rye whiskey. Why don't you try it?"

She brushed her hair back from her eyes. "Marshal Long, are you offering to buy me a drink? Because if you're not, I'm going to have to refuse. I was in such haste to get away from Robert that I didn't get to the bank and I'm very low on funds."

"Maybe I can help you."

She shook her head. "I have always paid my own way and I'm not about to change that policy now. I don't want to be beholden to anyone."

"I understand and greatly admire your strong sense of independence, Miss Danby."

"Really?"

"Oh yes," he assured her. "And frankly, I would have been surprised if you had accepted my money. But what I was proposing was a *loan*."

She sat down across the table from him, and he beckoned the waiter to bring her a glass. "Miss Danby, I would be happy to loan you some money. I don't have a lot of it, but I can wire for more and you could repay me or my office when we return to Denver."

"I doubt that I'll ever return to Denver."

Her answer puzzled him. "But don't you have . . . uh . . . things . . . that are important to you back there?"

"Not really," she said as the waiter brought her a glass, filled it, and refilled Longarm's glass before hurrying off. "I'm not a woman who cares for collecting possessions. My father was a traveling preacher in Illinois. During most of my early childhood we lived out of a wagon, and during winter and bad weather we were given shelter by whoever had Christian charity in their hearts."

"And your mother was fine with that kind of life?" he asked.

"Not really. She hated being on the move all the time and never being able to put down roots. My mother died when I was twelve years old. We were trying to sleep one freezing night in a . . . a barn. She caught pneumonia, and we did not have the money or luxury of good medical care."

"I'm sorry. Is that why you went into nursing?"

"It is," she confessed. "My father left me with relatives in Chicago and I was raised in a proper home by my uncle, who was a prosperous physician. I wanted to be a physician as well . . . but of course . . . that is still not acceptable in this country, so I became a nurse."

"And a very good one."

"I try to be. I really do. And I was very happy working at the hospital in Denver until I allowed myself to become romantically entangled with Robert Gaylord. I assure you, Marshal, it is a mistake that I will never, ever repeat."

Longarm raised his glass in a toast. "To your new beginning wherever that might be."

They touched glasses and drank their imported brandy, both turning to watch the light go rosy and the mesas north of the tracks gleam like polished copper in the dying light.

"How do you like the brandy?"

"Delicious, Marshal. Thank you very much."

"My name is Custis Long. Just call me Custis."

"And you may call me Laura."

"A lovely name for a lovely lady."

She blushed. "I have heard about you, and the talk was not one bit exaggerated. You really are a charmer."

"My appearance is not up to my normal high standards," he told her. "I appear as pale as a corpse. I'm sure you do not find me at all handsome."

She smiled but said nothing, and for a few moments, as the last light of day faded into darkness, they both held close their own private thoughts. The waiter refilled their glasses, and Longarm at last turned to Laura and said, "What did you have tonight to eat? The roast pork . . . or the delicious sage hen?"

"Actually, I didn't eat this evening. Not really hungry."

Longarm knew a lie when he heard one. "You didn't eat because you are broke," he said, signaling the waiter once more and saying, "The lady is ravenous. Could you please bring her both entrees?"

"Of course!"

"But. . . ." She tried a protest, but it wasn't very convincing. "Really, I'm not very hungry."

"Of course you're not. But I'm still a little hungry and we can share . . . can't we?"

"I'd like that," Laura told him.

"And I do insist on making a loan to you," he told her. "And if you really aren't returning to Denver, I can ask someone at my office to close your bank account and wire its funds to you in Flagstaff."

"You could actually do that?"

"We could," he said. "I'm sure that it would not be difficult to have that arranged as soon as we reach Arizona. After all, we are sworn officers of the law, and a telegram from you with specific banking instructions and your permission would suffice."

She brightened. "Thank you! I have three thousand dollars in my Denver account and I was so worried about returning. Now I don't have to!"

"Drink up," he said, pleased that she seemed so relieved and happy. "We will be in Flagstaff tomorrow morning."

"Is it pretty?"

"It's beautiful," he told her. "There are high peaks just north of town and great ponderosa forests, and lakes and streams.

"Is it far from the Grand Canyon?"

"A day's stage ride each way. They have a few little hotels at the South Rim and, I've heard, a saloon and café."

"I don't think that I'll be going to any saloon, but it's nice to know that they have accommodations."

"I'll loan you twenty-five dollars and you can repay me when your money is wired to Flagstaff," he told her.

"Custis, you'll never know how much I appreciate your kindness," she said. "I'm sure that there is no way that I can ever repay you."

"Oh, I can think of a way . . . but if I told you, you'd probably slap my poor old face."

She blushed again. "You really are something, Custis. Not a man that a good Christian woman could ever trust."

"You can trust me," he said, suddenly turning serious. "I've never taken advantage of any woman. I do have my own code of ethics, Nurse Laura, and it's one that I hold very high."

She sipped her brandy, eyes studying him thoughtfully. "I actually believe you."

"You should. Now, here comes our food. I do hope you are very hungry."

The waiter brought them two steaming platters heaped with pork, sage hen, carrots, and mashed potatoes, all swimming in a savory sauce.

"Oh my god," Laura whispered, grabbing up a napkin, knife, and fork. "This looks wonderful!"

"It is," Longarm said, puffing on his cigar and taking

great pleasure in watching the nurse who had possibly saved his life dig into the meal with so much gusto that it was painfully obvious she had been starving.

Later, they sat and sipped more brandy and talked about their lives and their hopes. Longarm discovered that this woman had a huge and generous heart. She was one of those people who felt it her destiny to help those less fortunate than herself. Laura Danby talked about places that she had worked and people whose lives she had helped through her profession.

"And you, Marshal Custis Long. You are also someone who believes that we are put on this earth to do more than simply accumulate wealth, power, or prestige."

"I am?"

"Of course you are!" she said, obviously a little tipsy from drink. "You are a knight of the American West. A man who risks his life to uphold the law and make sure that everyone is served with justice and honesty. I have already seen how gallantly you came to my rescue at the train station. Robert Gaylord, if he had not told you, was very skilled in the art of pugilism."

"He told me, and that's why I didn't give him a moment to even think about putting up a defense. I simply hit him as fast and hard as I could, and then when he fell, I showed him no mercy and gave him no quarter."

"He deserved none. But . . ."

"But what?" Longarm asked.

"I may never return to Denver . . . but *you* must. And when you do . . . I'm very worried that Dr. Gaylord might have a very unpleasant surprise waiting for you."

"I'll be all right," Longarm assured her. "If worse

came to worst, my boss could transfer me out of Denver to another federal office. And I have been offered many jobs that pay more than I make right now."

"So you have alternatives."

"Yes, I do. I think we all do, only sometimes we just don't see them, or we forget that they exist. No one likes change, but it can be all for the good."

"I like change," Laura Danby said. "I like to see new country, meet new people, and . . ."

"And what?"

"Even fall in love all over again. But that can be very dangerous for a lone woman in a man's West."

"Given your beauty," he said quite honestly, "it would be very dangerous for a man, too."

"You are a shameless flatterer."

"Maybe," he agreed. "But I might as well tell you that I have no idea of exiting your world after we get to Flagstaff."

She reached across the table and caressed his face. "I'm very glad to hear that."

Longarm felt a sudden desire for Nurse Laura Danby that was almost overpowering. But he knew that he had to move slowly with her . . . and he had already decided that he would do whatever was necessary in the short time given him to win her heart and loving affections.

Chapter 8

When they stepped off the train in Flagstaff, Longarm escorted Miss Danby a few blocks north to the Hotel Weatherford on Leroux Street. It was a fine-looking hotel, and Longarm knew that they had a special wing just for single women and that Laura would not bothered there by undesirable men.

"This is an impressive hotel," she said when they entered the spacious lobby. "But won't it be too expensive?"

"Not if I book the rooms at my government rate," he assured her.

Laura looked worried. "Custis, I appreciate all that you're doing for me, but I'm not going to . . ."

"I know. I know. But I'll be down at the end of the hall. And I promise you that I won't bother you in any way unless you *want* to be bothered."

"You *are* a gentleman. And as soon as I've taken my little excursion to see the Grand Canyon, I'll be visiting whatever they have here that serves as a hospital and applying for a job. If I'm successful, I'll look for a respectable boardinghouse where I can afford to stay on a longer term basis."

"It sounds like you've thought this out."

"I have." She paused a moment before he went to the registration desk. "And what will *you* be doing while I'm sightseeing and getting myself established here in Flagstaff?"

"As soon as I've unpacked and cleaned up a bit, I'll go find the local marshal and fill him in on Eli Pittman. Maybe he knows where I can find Pittman, and if that is the case, I'll go at once to arrest the man."

"Is he . . . dangerous?"

"Very." Longarm frowned. "Even my own boss told me that he's faster with a gun than I am. What I'll need to do is get the drop on him. Once I've done that, I can jail the man and think about returning him directly to Denver to face charges of attempted murder."

"I can't imagine myself going off to enjoy the majesty of the Grand Canyon while wondering if you are getting killed in the line of duty."

"I'll be fine."

She moved close to him and looked up into his face. "Maybe you are right and it will all go as you hope. But, Custis, I saved your skin not too long ago at Cherry Creek, and I'd hate so see all that time and effort go to waste now that we've come all the way to Flagstaff."

"I can't let you go with me. You've had a long trip and I know you're tired. You slept in a chair while I slept on a bed . . . well, not much of one, but at least I was able to stretch out."

"I stretched out in my chair and slept. And I really can't just go off sightseeing while you are risking your life."

Longarm bent and kissed her forehead. "Seems that we have an impasse here, Laura. Any ideas?"

"I *always* have ideas," she told him. "How about I sort of shadow you when you go to see the local authorities? And afterward, shadow you some more until I'm sure that you are not in danger."

He almost laughed, but there were a lot of people in the fine hotel lobby and Longarm had no wish to attract their curiosity or attention. "Laura," he said, steering her off to a corner of the room where their words could not be overheard. "Do you realize that I've *never* been shadowed by anyone in my entire life unless they were waiting to kill me."

"Well, I mean to see that you are safe, and so my protective shadowing is different."

"But what would be the point?"

"The point would be," she told him very seriously, "that if you were shot, I would be close and might be able to save your life. And if you have to shoot Marshal Pittman, perhaps my presence would save his life."

"If I am forced to shoot first, there isn't anything you or anyone else on this earth could do to save Pittman's life. I always shoot to kill."

"I'm following you," she said, chin lifting stubbornly. "Now, we can do this as a team or as individuals. But one thing I can tell you for certain is that I am not going off to see one of the great wonders of the world while fretting about your life!"

"I could easily give you the slip," he told her. "I'm good at that when the job requires it."

"Then I'd simply go to the local authorities, tell them why you are here, and we'd all wait for your arrival."

Longarm swore under his breath. "Laura Danby, you have to be the most stubborn, pigheaded woman I've ever come across."

"Thank you," she said, smiling sweetly. "I'll take that as a compliment."

"It wasn't meant to be a compliment."

"Doesn't matter. Why don't we just get registered for tonight and then go find the authorities and find out what the next step will be?"

Longarm wanted to reach out and wring her pretty neck, but instead he kissed her full on the lips. She did not slap him as he halfway expected, but instead kissed him back.

"Now," she said, "we've got that much accomplished. Can we just get registered and get on with business?"

"Why not?" he asked.

Thirty minutes later they met back down in the lobby. Laura had brushed her hair and managed to freshen up. She was quite the looker, and men turned their heads in admiration.

Longarm offered her his arm, but she refused. "Remember? I'm going to shadow you."

"I don't like being shadowed."

"Get used to it until we find out about this terrible Marshal Pittman."

"I think you can safely assume that he's no longer a deputy United States marshal."

"He'll still have his badge, won't he?"

"Yes, but . . ."

"Then all he has to do is show it and say he's a marshal and anyone would take his word for that, wouldn't they?"

"Yes, but . . ."

"All right then," she said, "get moving. I'll just sort of mosey along a half block behind. And when you come out of the marshal's office, don't try to lose me."

"I wouldn't dream of it."

"I'm hungry and I want you to buy me dinner and I still haven't gotten that twenty-five dollars you offered as a loan."

He fished out the money and looked down at her with affection. "We'll go to the telegraph office, wire Denver, and get the ball rolling to empty your account."

"That sounds like an excellent idea. I don't like being beholden, even to someone as kind as yourself. And so the sooner I have my own funds, the better I'll feel about things."

"I'd already guessed that," he said.

Longarm glanced up and down the street, thinking that this woman wasn't easy and she had a tendency to be a mite bossy, but she genuinely was concerned for his welfare and that felt good. If he were shot by Eli Pittman, he had no doubt that she was the kind of friend who would pick the gun out of his dead hand and try to kill Pittman herself.

There wasn't any equivocation in the way that Nurse Laura Danby saw things. She was pretty much a black-or-white, wrong-or-right thinker, and he liked that because he was the same way himself.

"Can you shoot a gun?" he asked as they started up Leroux Street.

"Of course I can. And I can hit what I aim at most of the time."

"You need a gun to carry in your purse, Laura."

"I have one," she said, surprising him. "A two-shot derringer. It's a cute little thing, and although I've never had to fire it, I'm sure it would put two very big holes in anyone that I shot."

"I'm sure that it would," he said, pointing up ahead. "There's the marshal's office."

"And there is a nice little candy store. I've got a few dollars. Do you like chocolate?"

"I'd die for good dark chocolate."

"Don't you dare," she said, giving his arm a squeeze. "And I'll be sitting inside the candy store at one of those little tables eating your chocolate, so don't dillydally or it will be all gone."

"Wouldn't dream of it," Longarm said with a chuckle as he headed off toward the Flagstaff Marshal's Office.

Chapter 9

Longarm read the crude wooden sign on a paint-peeling door that said, "MARSHAL BUFORD BEAR." He then stepped inside the office and looked around, not surprised to see that Marshal Bear was absent. Most small town marshals were poorly paid, and many didn't even have the funds to hire a low-paid deputy or assistant. From the looks of this office, Buford Bear was operating on a very thin budget. There was one windowless cell butted up against the back wall, and it contained nothing but a straw mattress resting a rough pine bed frame. In another corner was a battered and soot-covered potbellied stove that had seen far better days. A scarred desk looked off balance, with one broken leg and the rest propped up on bricks, and there was a waste bucket spilling bean cans and empty tobacco tins to the floor. Cigarette and cigar butts were piled up in a dented milk can that served as a combination ash tray and spittoon.

There were two chairs, and since Longarm had nothing better to do for the moment, he took a seat and laced his hands behind his head. When his eyes turned upward, he saw that the ceiling's corners were latticed with cobwebs.

"Buford Bear might be one hell of a good marshal, but he sure isn't big on neatness or cleanliness," Longarm said to himself. "Place smells like a stable or a saloon."

Longarm didn't see any Wanted posters tacked to the walls, and Marshal Bear's desk was covered with old newspapers and dime novels. Putting it all together, Longarm had the feeling that Buford Bear was not going to be very professional.

He must have dozed off for a while, because he was suddenly awakened by the slamming of the front door and then a howl of pain as a huge man hurled a drunken man headfirst into the room, making him slide into the cell bars. Before the drunk could even scramble to his feet, the big man booted him in the ass, causing his head to crash against the cell bars.

"Ahhhh!" the man shouted, curling up in a ball.

Longarm saw the glint of a silver badge on the giant's chest and knew this was Marshal Bear.

"Marshal," Longarm said, jumping out of his chair and placing himself between the prisoner and the marshal. "Don't you think that he's had enough of a beating?"

The man was huge, at least three inches taller than Longarm, who stood an impressive six-three in his stockings. And Buford Bear was immense, probably weighing close to three hundred pounds. His face was covered with a thick black beard, and his legs were as big around as the trunks of most pine trees. The Colt revolver the town marshal wore on his hip looked like a toy.

"Who the hell are you!" Bear growled, forgetting about the moaning drunk that was sobbing on his dirty floor.

"I'm Deputy United States Marshal Custis Long."

Bear blinked. "Got any proof of it?"

Longarm dutifully produced his badge, and Bear took it into his big hand. He had an overhanging brow and great big bushy eyebrows with wild hairs that shot out in all directions. All in all, the town marshal looked slightly insane.

"Hmmmm," Bear mused. "Looks authentic."

"It *is* authentic."

"What are you doin' in my office?"

"I was waiting to speak with you," Longarm told the giant. He glanced down at the man writhing on the floor. "I think you might have hurt him pretty bad. Probably needs a doctor."

"The only thing that miserable bastard needs right now is a bottle of rotgut whiskey. Elmer, crawl into that cell! You know the way 'cause you've been there enough times!"

Elmer whimpered, and before he could move, Marshal Bear grabbed him by the ankles and dragged him into the cell, then slammed and locked it tight. The drunk kept moaning, and Longarm could see that his face was battered and both eyes were swelled shut.

"Did you do that to Elmer?" Longarm asked, his voice edged with disgust and anger.

"Nope. If I'd have done it, he'd be lookin' a whole lot

worse than he does right now. You see Elmer . . . in addition to being the town drunk . . . is also a petty thief and a general nuisance to everyone . . . most especially myself."

"He's still a human being, Marshal Bear. And from what I can see . . . he needs to be seen by a doctor."

"You payin' for the doctorin'?" Bear demanded. "Because, if you ain't . . . then you better keep your mouth shut. I don't have any money for doctors, and this drunken bastard is usin' up this month's prisoner food money so fast I won't have any left for whoever else I arrest."

"Sounds like the town council has you on a pretty short tether," Longarm remarked, trying to curb his temper. "But I didn't come here to talk money, Marshal Bear."

Bear's mind jumped around like a cricket in a hot frying pan. "How much does the federal government pay you a month?"

"What?"

"You heard me," Bear snapped. "I want to know how much money you make every month."

"That's none of your business."

The giant's lips turned into a sneer. "Yeah, it is! I'm a taxpayer. And you know what I make here? Thirty lousy dollars a month! Thirty dollars! Why a saloon swamper in Flagstaff makes that much. Even an *ugly* whore can hump up a hundred! But not me. I risk my life every day and they pay me thirty dollars and I get one damned meal at the worst café in town. And in that café I can only eat the daily special, which ain't worth dry dog shit!"

Longarm could see that this man was really getting himself worked up. "Marshal, my advice would be to quit and find a better job."

"I like what I do here," Bear shot back as he flopped into his protesting office chair and kicked his boots up on his desk. "And I do get to sleep in this shit hole of an office, so I don't have to pay no hotel room rent."

"Well," Longarm said, trying desperately to turn the conversation around and then remove himself before he lost his temper and spoke his mind, "things are hard all over right now."

Bear wasn't listening. His brain was still fixed on the injustice of his salary compared to that of a federal officer of the law. "What did you say your name was?"

"I didn't say, but it's Custis Long."

"Well, Long, I'll bet the federal government pays you at least seventy-five dollars a month." Bear's eyes narrowed and he pointed a finger at Longarm. Ain't that right?"

"Close," Longarm said, realizing that this man had his mind locked on badgering him about his salary and it was going to take a miracle just to get him off the subject.

"That's what I thought!" Bear shouted. "Why, Marshal Long, you make more'n twice as much as me! And you get to sashay around the country here and there playing the important man. Where you from?"

"I work out of Denver."

"And I'll bet you didn't ride in the cheap train car with the scum of the earth, did you?"

"No."

"No." Buford Bear shook his head. "Hell no, you

didn't ride in the cheap car. You had a sleeping car and you ate in the train's fancy dining car."

"That's right, Marshal. I did. But now that we've gone over all the luxuries that I get on the job, I need to ask you a question."

"Shoot."

"I've come all the way from Denver to find and arrest a man named Eli Pittman. Do you know where I can find him?"

Buford Bear's eyes were black and sunk deep under those beetle brows. "What did he do?"

"He almost killed my boss and he tried to kill me."

"Eli Pittman shot you and your boss?"

"That's right."

"I can't rightly believe that," Buford Bear said, smiling for the first time.

"And why not?"

"Because I know Eli Pittman, and he's the best man I ever saw with a gun. Better'n me, even. And he *never* misses what he aims at."

"Well," Longarm said. "He shot up my boss, Marshal Billy Vail, and damn near killed him. And he would have killed me, but I jumped out of a second-story window and got away."

"Through glass," Bear said, grinning. "That's why your hands are so cut up."

"Yeah," Longarm said. "Now where can I find Eli Pittman?"

"Be damned if I know. He was in town a few days ago, but he ain't no more. Said he was a United States marshal lookin' to arrest or shoot the man who nearly killed our territorial governor."

"Pittman isn't a federal law officer anymore," Longarm told the man. "And I need to find and arrest him."

"Good luck," Buford Bear said. "Eli has a lot of friends and family in Northern Arizona. If you find him, you'll have a whole damned army of men that you'll have to take down first."

"Where do I start searching?" Longarm asked.

"Damned if I know."

"Where the hell is his family?" Longarm snapped.

"They are here in Flagstaff, some in Williams, more in Prescott." Bear stood up, and he wasn't smiling anymore. "Like I said, the man has family all over this territory."

"Damn," Longarm muttered.

Buford Bear hitched his big thumbs into his suspenders. "And I'm going to tell you one other thing that you'll find out sooner rather than later."

"And that would be?"

"Eli Pittman is my cousin."

Longarm audibly groaned. "So you're not going to help me at all, are you?"

"I'll help you, Marshal Custis Long. I'll help you straight to the train station for the first one out of here." Buford Bear yanked a cheap brass pocket watch out of his pocket. "Leaves in about three hours, and you got lucky, because it's the eastbound."

"I'm not going anywhere until I find and either arrest or kill Eli Pittman."

"Then you might as well stop by the mortuary when you leave this office and tell the man that owns it what you want engraved on your headstone."

Longarm went to the door. "So that's the way it's going to be around here?"

"Yep."

Longarm nodded. "All right. I won't expect any help from you, Marshal Bear. But if you get between me and Eli Pittman, I'll not hesitate to take you down."

"You just keep flappin' your lips, Marshal Long. And spend that big paycheck as fast as you can this month, because you may not live to see another."

Longarm opened the door and said, "You're a pig and a disgrace to our profession. No wonder you can't find a better job."

Buford Bear cursed and jumped out of his chair, but by then Longarm was already out the door and heading for the candy shop.

Chapter 10

"Dark fudge chocolate with pecans," Laura said, smacking her lips and pointing to a large serving still resting on the plate. "You don't know how hard it was for me not to devour your half."

Longarm had a sour taste in his mouth after his visit with Marshal Bear. He reached down and broke off a small piece of the fudge and shoved it into his mouth. "Delicious."

"You don't *sound* like you think it's very delicious," Laura said, looking disappointed. "What's the matter?"

Longarm gave her a quick rundown on his unpleasant meeting with the town marshal and ended by saying, "Buford Bear even suggested that I get on the first train out of Flagstaff or I might not live to spend another paycheck."

"He said *that*?"

"Yep. He even admitted that Eli Pittman is his cousin."

"Oh, shit," she whispered.

"My sentiment exactly," Longarm replied. "What this

means is that not only will I not get any local help or support, but Marshal Bear is going to become a very big thorn in my side. He might even try to have me . . . removed."

Her eyes widened with alarm. "You mean that Marshal Bear might try to kill you!"

"That's right. He's a giant of a man, probably as slow-witted as he is slow moving, but he'll have a lot of friends around here and I'm sure that he carries a good deal of influence in this town. So you see, Laura, I've not been here two hours and already the deck is stacking up against me."

"It certainly seems to be," she agreed. "Well, what are we going to do next?"

" '*We*' ?" he echoed.

"That's right. You don't expect that I'm going to go sightseeing at the Grand Canyon and leave you all alone here in Flagstaff? Uh-uh! Not for a minute I'm not."

"Listen," Longarm said, taking another nibble of the dark chocolate fudge, "I'm very touched by and appreciative of your offer, but I can't allow you to be involved in this mess."

"And why not?"

"It's going to be dangerous!" He lowered his voice when the shop owner whirled around to stare. "Don't you understand that everyone in this town might line up against us?"

Laura Danby thought about that for a moment, and as usual, she had a solution. "Then why don't we just leave this town?"

"And why would we do that?"

She shrugged. "Well, if Eli Pittman isn't in Flagstaff,

why would we want to stay here when the marshal and at least half the town is in cahoots against us?"

"Good point," Longarm conceded. "Have you ever thought of going into detective work?"

"The Pinkerton Agency doesn't hire women agents and neither do local law enforcement officers. And I'm sure that your federal office hasn't employed any female marshals.

"Nope."

"So you see that if I tried to get a job as a marshal or detective, I'd get nowhere in that man's world. Besides, I do enjoy being a nurse, as long as I don't have to fight off amorous doctors."

"I'm glad you explained things." Longarm scowled. "I guess that the next thing to do is to find out if Pittman is in Flagstaff and, if not, where he is most likely to have gone."

"That sounds entirely reasonable. Where do we start looking?"

Longarm said, "I'll hit the saloons and the livery stables, because I've always found them to be rich sources of local gossip and information. How about you going to the newspaper office and striking up a conversation with the editor or a young reporter, who will almost certainly be flummoxed and dazzled by your striking good looks?"

She batted her eyelashes across the table. "Are you suggesting that I . . . I *flirt* with some poor editor or reporter in order to gain information?"

"If that is what it takes, sure." Longarm glanced out the window. "And for today at least, it would be better if you are not seen with me."

"And why is that?"

"If Marshal Bear knows we are together, he'll be watching. If you go to the newspaper office, he might even be smart enough to think that you are looking for information to help me find Pittman. He could come down hard on anyone there who gave you information about Pittman. So it's just better all the way around if he doesn't realize we are together right away."

"I see what you mean. But I'm sure he'll discover that we've both checked into the Weatherford Hotel."

"But not in the same room. For all he knows, we simply came in on the train and went to the most popular hotel."

"But surely he'll see a connection."

Longarm nodded. "He will, but maybe not until tomorrow."

"All right then," she said, standing up. "You owe the man fifty cents for the chocolate fudge, Custis. I'm going to find the newspaper office and see what I can learn about Marshal Pittman."

"Just refer to him as Eli Pittman and make up some story about your being a friend or distant relative."

Her eyebrows shot up with disapproval. "But that would be a bald-faced lie!"

"I'm pretty certain that God will forgive you, and so will I," Longarm said dryly as he chucked fifty cents down and added, "You should leave right now. I'll wait about five minutes and we can meet up this evening in the hotel's dining room."

"Seven o'clock?"

"That will be fine," he told her. "If I'm late, just go ahead and order your meal and I'll be along as soon after as I can."

"But if you don't come, then *I'll* have to pay for the meal?"

"I'll take care of that," he promised. "Charge it to my room if I'm late."

"No strings attached?"

Longarm winked. "Laura, there are never any free meals in this life. Everything good comes at a price."

"And what would that be?" she asked demurely.

"We can talk about that tonight."

"Maybe we will, but maybe not. Depends."

"On what?"

"I don't know," she admitted. "I'll have to think about this very hard."

"Think about finding out if Pittman is still in Flagstaff or not," Longarm told her. "And I'll do the same."

Nurse Laura Danby smiled, and as she went out the door she whispered, "This is almost going to be fun."

After she was gone, Longarm shook his head and took his seat at the table. He was feeling a little better about things, and Laura's good spirits and enthusiasm was a tonic. So he finished off the last of the fudge and then lit a cigar and smoked in thoughtful silence for a while before he left to find out if Eli Pittman was still in town.

And if he was, this might be the day that one or the other of them died.

Chapter 11

Longarm knew that it was a bit too early in the day for most men to be drinking in saloons, so he decided to go to the livery stables first. In a town this size you could expect that there would be only two or three. Over the years he had found that livery owners were often talkative and eager to share information, especially if they thought you were interested in buying a horse and saddle.

And, Longarm thought, he might just have to buy a couple of horses and saddles, courtesy of the United States government, if Pittman had left town. Usually, when Longarm did so, it was with the explicit understanding that he could return the tack and animal at about seventy or eighty percent of its purchase price. But there had been times when he'd used a horse so hard during a manhunt that he'd gotten only half the money he'd paid just a short time earlier.

"Afternoon!" he called when he walked into Pilgrim's Stable and looked around in the murky light for someone. "Anyone here?"

"Sure am!" a sleepy voice called back to him from up in a loft filled with hay. "Can I help you?"

"Maybe."

"I'll be right on down," the man said, hitching up his suspenders, slapping hay off of himself, and then descending on a rickety ladder. "Name is Moses Pilgrim. I own this stable and I rent and sell good horses, mules, burros, and wagons. What will be your pleasure today?"

Longarm liked a man who came right to the point. "Well, I might need a horse and then again I might not."

Pilgrim frowned and looked perplexed. "You sayin' that you don't even know if you need a horse or not?"

"Yeah," Longarm replied, "that's about the size of it."

"Well, when will you know if you need or horse or not?"

"Maybe after we talk a bit."

"Then talk," Moses Pilgrim urged, stifling a yawn. "I got the time to listen."

Rather than be devious, Longarm decided to lay his cards faceup on the table. "I'm a United States marshal out of Denver looking for a man named Eli Pittman. Have you heard of him?"

"I might have," Pilgrim said guardedly. "Why you lookin' for Eli?"

"He shot my boss down and almost killed me. I'm looking to arrest him and take him back to Denver to stand trial."

Pilgrim plucked a piece of hay out of his hair, stuck it between his teeth, and chewed it thoughtfully. "Marshal, you don't look like you were almost killed."

"Oh, but I was," Longarm said. "Eli was a United

States marshal the same as myself and that's how he got the drop on us back in Denver."

"And why would he do that?"

"It's a long story," Longarm said evasively.

"Well now," Pilgrim said, chewing furiously on the stem of hay, "I seem to recall that when Eli drew his gun and pulled the trigger, no one he ever aimed at lived. And here you are telling me that not only did you live but so did your boss."

"Sometimes luck strikes twice, and that's what happened in our case. Listen, Mr. Pilgrim, I'm not interested in involving you in any way. But if Pittman is still in Flagstaff, I'm trusting that you'll tell me so, in order that I can do my sworn duty."

"And if I told you he left Flagstaff?"

"Then I'd probably want to buy a couple of horses and have you point me toward his destination."

"Why a 'couple of horses'?"

"Because I've got a lady friend that is riding with me."

Moses Pilgrim shook his head. "My oh my! So a United States marshal is dragging along a woman to help him catch and arrest Eli?"

Longarm knew how lame that sounded, so he just shrugged his shoulders as if to say the situation was not entirely of his choosing. "If I buy two horses from you, it will mean more of a profit . . . providing you agree to buy them and their saddles back after I return."

"If you're after Eli Pittman, the odds are that neither you nor the woman will return."

"Then you make an even better profit," Longarm told the man. "So are you going to tell me anything, or do I go to another stable and find out what I need to know and profit some other liveryman?"

Pilgrim actually smiled around the stem of hay bobbing from his lips. "You're a smart man, Marshal. I'll hand that much to you. You take along a woman and you understand how to convince a simple fella like me to tell you what you want to know. Not even half-dumb, I'd say."

Longarm was getting a bit impatient. "Let's quit squirreling around and get to the point. Is Eli Pittman still in Flagstaff? And you'd damn sure better not lie to me, Mr. Pilgrim."

Pilgrim threw up his big, rough hands as if defending himself. "Oh, I wouldn't dream of lying to a federal marshal! As far as I know, Eli skipped town several days ago. He wasn't here long. Just came, stayed a few nights, got drunk and rowdy, and left early one morning."

"Where did Pittman go?"

"Hell if I know."

"Guess."

Pilgrim frowned. "Eli has a lot of friends and family down around Prescott. If I was looking for him . . . which I'm glad that I am not . . . I'd ride for Prescott. And when I got there, I'd be real quiet and careful about who I asked and what questions I asked. I'd try my damnedest to catch Eli in town when he was dead drunk. That would be my best chance of surviving. Yep, that would be my only chance, but I can tell you that even drunk, Eli Pittman is hell on wheels and deadly with a gun, knife, or rifle."

"Okay," Longarm said, turning to leave. "Thanks for the information. I'm going to trust that you haven't lied to me. That you're not related to Eli and aren't his friend."

"I'm not either of them things," Pilgrim vowed passionately. "I've always stayed as far away from Eli and his bunch as possible. If you should somehow manage to arrest or kill the son of a bitch, I'll drink to you, Marshal. But you had better understand that Marshal Buford Bear is Eli's cousin and they get along pretty damn well."

"That's the impression I got when I visited the marshal's office."

"Well, it's true. And whenever Eli goes on a tear, Marshal Bear just waits until he's falling down drunk and then carries him off to a whorehouse or hotel. He never arrests Eli like he does anyone else who misbehaves. So if you get Eli, Buford will be gunning for you."

"I already figured that out after visiting the marshal's office," Longarm said. "But your telling me confirms that you're an honest and straightforward man."

"So you want to go out back and look over a couple of good horses I have for sale?"

"Maybe tomorrow."

"Why wait?"

Longarm smiled and waved good-bye. "I want to talk to some more people about Eli."

"Nothin' they can tell you that I haven't already said."

"Probably not," Longarm replied. "But I still want to talk to a few more people."

"Just watch your back and watch out for your woman! I want your business tomorrow."

Longarm just smiled as he headed up the street to talk to more people and make sure that he had gotten the full and straight story from Moses Pilgrim.

* * *

Three hours later in the Salty Dog Saloon, Longarm was nursing his second beer and feeling his stomach growl for solid food. He'd been to three saloons before this one, and in every establishment he'd pretty much gotten the same story and warnings as he'd received from Moses Pilgrim.

In this saloon, however, he was getting the strong and unpleasant feeling that he was in enemy territory. Here the drinkers weren't talking loud or laughing or behaving like normal saloon customers. Rather, they were sullen and mostly silent since he'd let his purpose and his official status be known.

Longarm set his mug of beer down on the bar and turned to face the six or seven grim-faced men. He was feeling a little grim himself and itching to scratch some bark off these unfriendly people.

"So," he said loudly, "I'm getting the feeling that I'm not all that welcome here in the Salty Dog Saloon. And I have to say I don't mind that even one little bit. The beer is piss, the place stinks like a hog's pen, and you fellas look like you are all inbred, but other than that, I'm fine with being here."

One man, big and angry-faced, pointed his finger at Longarm and shouted, "Do you know who the hell I am?"

"Nope. Who are you, Mr. Big Mouth?"

"I'm Elias Pittman. I'm Eli's younger brother, and gawdamn if I like you here among me and my friends."

"Well gawdamn if I give a salty shit," Longarm said with a grin, while wondering if he could goad this man into revealing something of importance. "If you're Eli's brother, then maybe you can tell me why he is such a miserable coward."

Elias snorted like a bull and balled his fists. "If you weren't wearing a badge, Marshal, I'd kick your ass all over town then I'd stomp you to death like a stray dog."

Elias was big and he was probably a tough fighter. But he wasn't wearing a sidearm and he was drunk. Also, his friends didn't look nearly as interested in tangling with a United States marshal.

"So where is your brother?" Longarm asked. "Is he hiding like the coward I know him to be?"

"He ain't hidin' from nobody! He's no coward, and he'd kill you if he were in this saloon right now."

"Oh," Longarm said, a tight smile on his lips, "your brother already tried to do that a while ago in Denver. But as you can plainly see . . . he failed. Now I'm going to arrest him for the attempted murder of two federal law officers. He won't swing from the gallows, but I expect that he'll be so old by the time he gets his release from prison that he'll have to gum soft corn in order to stay alive."

Elias Pittman bellowed a curse and charged along the bar. Longarm waited until exactly the right moment, and then he grabbed his heavy beer mug and smashed Elias right between the eyes. He broke the man's nose, clouded his eyes with blood and beer, and deftly stepped out of his runaway path. Elias stumbled, and Longarm jumped up behind the man and kicked him right between his legs so hard that Elias screamed in agony and bent over double. Longarm stepped around the man, grabbed another beer mug, and laid it across Elias's head so hard that he dropped like a heavy stone and just quivered on the sawdust-covered floor, moaning and groaning.

Longarm stepped back and glared at the other frozen customers. "Who is next?"

They all retreated a step, and Longarm laughed coldly. "A fine bunch of friends you are! I just kicked the shit out of Elias, and you boys look like you're ready to piss your pants and run."

They didn't say a word. Longarm tossed a nickel on the bar and headed outside. He drew in a deep breath and decided that Moses Pilgrim had given him about as much information as he was likely to get in Flagstaff. Now he was hungry and ready for a nice and maybe even memorable evening with Nurse Laura Danby.

Longarm started up the street at a leisurely pace. He pulled out his pocket watch, which had a derringer attached to the fob, and the watch told him that it was almost seven-thirty. He was going to be a bit late, and he was eager to find out if Laura had been able to gain any additional information at the local newspaper. If he were a betting man, he would bet that she had charmed some poor scribe into telling her everything he knew or had ever known about Eli Pittman.

But just as he was rounding the corner onto Leroux Street, a movement caught the corner of his eye and then he saw a flash of gunfire. Longarm threw himself down on the boardwalk, drew his gun, and fired in one less than two heartbeats. But he saw his bullet splinter a wooden building and knew that he'd missed.

Jumping up, Longarm sprinted toward where he had

caught a glimpse of the would-be assassin. No one was in sight.

Holstering his gun and deciding that there was no chance of finding out who had tried to ambush him, Longarm headed up the street walking a little faster. He was hungry both for good food and the company of Nurse Danby . . . although not in that particular order.

Chapter 12

When Longarm entered the dining room located on the main floor of the elegant Hotel Weatherford, he saw Laura waving at him from a table set in the far corner.

"Wait until you hear what I've learned," she said with unconcealed excitement as he took his place at the small, round table draped in white linen and with a vase filled with fresh red roses on it.

Longarm had already decided not to tell her about someone trying to ambush him just a few minutes earlier, because they would be leaving in the morning and he did not want to place any more stress on Laura. It was his opinion that whoever had tried to bushwhack him might come after them, but most likely not.

"So what did you learn?" he asked, pouring himself a glass of wine and forcing himself to relax and listen.

"I met the nicest man at the newspaper office. His name is Dan Berryhill, and he is the owner, editor, and publisher. He was very cooperative when I told him that I was distantly related to Eli Pittman."

"And I suppose he was young, single, and good-looking?"

"How did you guess?"

Longarm shrugged. "What did Mr. Berryhill tell you?"

"He began by saying that he could hardly imagine that someone like me would be related to Mr. Pittman. But when I assured him that I was very, very distantly related, he warmed up considerably. It seems that Eli's father and mother have a cattle ranch about twenty-five miles west of here. I learned that it's not a big or prosperous ranch, but it is profitable and they also have a sawmill, which is quite profitable."

"That's quite interesting," Longarm said. "Did Mr. Berryhill think that is where Eli went when he left Flagstaff?"

"No," Laura said. "The rumor is that the territorial governor is related to the Pittmans and that Eli thinks he can somehow get an important government job in Prescott. Something like the head of the state militia or Rangers or something."

"I didn't even know that Arizona had a militia, but they do have Rangers." Longarm scowled. "Did you find out anything more?"

"Yes. It seems that Pittman has a wife."

Longarm's jaw dropped. "A wife?"

"Uh-huh. He married her last year and she is related to the territorial governor. That's Pittman's hole card and the reason he thinks he can gain a high office down in Prescott."

"I'm wondering if Pittman's wife lives here in Flagstaff," Longarm mused. "If she does, we need to see her."

"I was told that she lives in Prescott. Mr. Berryhill

said that Rachel is a real spitfire and quite a beauty. I guess it was quite a coup when Eli won her hand."

"But then he went to Denver and to work for the federal government," Longarm said. "So why would a man leave a beautiful bride and the promise of a high office in Arizona?"

"I have no idea."

"Did Berryhill mention if the couple had any children?"

"He said that they didn't have any children, just lots of low-life relatives."

Longarm pushed his wine aside and signaled the waiter. "Whiskey," he ordered.

When it arrived, Longarm drank his whiskey neat. He frowned, leaned forward, and grumbled, "Things don't seem to be shaping up in my favor, Laura."

"Why is that? I thought with all this new information you'd be very pleased."

"Let's review what we've learned," Longarm told her. "We now know that Eli Pittman's parents have a ranch west of here with a profitable sawmill. So that means that there is money in the family and there are at least a few employees. And, make no mistake about it, those employees will *not* consider us friends when they learn that we intend to arrest Eli."

"Yes, but—"

"We'll deal with that," Longarm interrupted. "I've already had the misfortune of meeting one of Eli's younger brothers, and the meeting did not end with hugs and best wishes."

"Did you . . . hurt him?"

"You could say that," Longarm told her. "The man

was drunk and spoiling for a fight. I obliged him, and he was not feeling well when I walked out of the Salty Dog Saloon."

"But you didn't kill him," Laura said, looking very worried.

"No. Elias was drunk and angry enough to have killed me if he'd gotten me down on the floor, but I never gave him a chance. Still, I'll bet that as soon as he can get up and ride, he'll be headed for the family ranch to warn his parents that I'm coming."

"And Eli might be hiding at his parents' ranch."

"I think it is far more likely that Eli is on his way to Prescott with the idea of talking his father-in-law into giving him some plum job with the territorial government."

"Why don't we just avoid the family ranch if you think that Eli isn't even there? Why risk another confrontation with Elias or any other angry members of the Pittman clan?"

"Because Prescott is one hell of a lot farther from here than the Pittman ranch and sawmill. I can't take the chance that Eli is holed up with his parents."

"I could find out if he's there."

"How?"

"I sure can't use the same story that I used on Dan Berryhill," she mused out loud. "But I could say that I had met Eli once before and was wondering if he was around."

"That might work," Longarm conceded. "I could stay hidden but within sight of the ranch. If Eli should happen to be hiding in the ranch house . . . you'd ride out fast and tell me."

"That sounds like a good plan," Laura said. "And now that I've told you what I found out at the newspaper office, I'm curious to learn what you learned in the saloons and at the livery stables."

"Not as much as you did." Longarm briefly recounted his afternoon and the warnings he'd received.

"And that's it?" she asked, looking a bit disappointed.

"Well," he said, deciding to tell her the rest, "someone also tried to ambush me just before I entered this hotel."

"Right out front in the street?"

"Yep. But they missed, and by the time I ran to where they'd been hiding, they were long gone."

"Whoever did it might be waiting for another chance when we leave tomorrow morning."

"I've thought of that and maybe we'll go out the back way. We need to buy supplies before we leave Flagstaff. I met a liveryman that I liked and think is trustworthy. We'll purchase our horses and saddles from him."

"The sooner we leave the better."

"I agree. Can you ride a horse?"

"Of course." Laura made a face. "How far is Prescott from here?"

"At least eighty miles."

"Custis, that's a *long* ride."

He decided that she wasn't much of a rider after all and said, "Perhaps we'll get lucky and find Eli Pittman at his parents' ranch."

She considered that a few minutes. "I almost hope not. Don't you think that things could get very . . . very difficult if you try to arrest the man with his family and friends around?"

"Yes," Longarm agreed. "But the sooner I find Eli and arrest him, the better I'll feel. He nearly killed my boss, and the only reason I'm still alive is that I got lucky and didn't break my fool neck when I threw myself through my upstairs window."

Their food looked delicious and they began to eat in silence, both of them considering the troubles the next day might bring.

"Laura?"

"Yes?"

Longarm chose his next words carefully. "Given what we've learned and what might lie ahead, don't you think it would be better if you went sightseeing at the Grand Canyon?"

"Is that what you want?"

"No," he admitted, "but it sure would be safer. And you've already been a huge help getting that information from Mr. Berryhill."

"Thank you."

"I have a feeling that Berryhill might like to be right here with you tomorrow night having dinner and drinks."

She smiled. "Oh, do you now?"

"Sure. And maybe you should see if that is going to happen."

"But then I'd have to continually wonder if you were alive or dead. I'd be so worried that I wouldn't have any appetite and I'd be unable to sleep. In short, Custis, I'd be a mess."

"You'd worry that much about me?"

"Yes, I would."

Longarm studied her lovely face for a few moments then made a decision. "Given all the danger we face here in Flagstaff, why don't you come to my room and spend the night?"

"For my safety, or yours?"

He laughed. "I wasn't thinking about 'safety,' Laura. I was thinking that if everything went wrong tomorrow at the Pittmans' ranch, then I'd be wishing that I had made love to you on my last night."

Tears sprang into her eyes and she reached out across the table to take his big hand. "That is such a *terrible* thought!"

"Not the part about making love to you."

Nurse Laura Danby stared down at her plate for a moment, obviously trying to come to a very important decision. Finally, she looked up and said, "Custis, there is something you need to know."

"Keep talking."

"I'm not a virgin, but I haven't slept with a man since I slept with my childhood sweetheart in Chicago almost eight years ago."

Longarm could not hide his surprise. "You've been . . . been chaste for *eight years*?"

"Yes. And Herman was the only one that ever knew me . . . intimately. So what I'm trying to tell you is that I'm afraid of physically being hurt, and I'm also worried that I will prove to be a monumental disappointment in your bed."

"That is quite a confession, Laura. But you know what?"

"What?"

"I'll be gentle, not rough. Slow, not fast. Mindful of your pleasure, not just my own. And I will *not* be disappointed in you. Of that much I am very sure."

Fresh tears spilled from the corners of her eyes. "Hurry up and finish your meal, Custis, before I change my mind and lose my nerve."

"I don't think you're capable of losing your nerve, but let's eat fast. We're going to need our strength tonight."

She laughed, until she realized that he was serious.

In the wee hours of the morning, Longarm carefully mounted Laura for the third time. He used his well-practiced and well-muscled body to pleasure her in the most exquisite way, bringing the nurse to another climax that made her toes tingle for the longest time.

"We are going to be pretty tired when we mount up and ride for Prescott in a few hours," she said, stifling a yawn.

"Do you have any regrets about tonight?"

Laura hugged his neck. "Not a one."

"I'm glad to hear that, but I still think you should go sightseeing at the Grand Canyon."

"I can do that any old time. And besides, how long has it been since *you've* seen the Grand Canyon?"

"It's been at least seven years."

"Then maybe after this is over we can go see it together."

Longarm nodded. He very much doubted that he'd have the time to revisit the Grand Canyon. If he managed to kill Eli Pittman, then Billy Vail would order him to hurry back to Denver. And if he didn't survive . . . well, what was the point in even making future plans?

"Custis?"

He yawned. There were probably only a few hours

left until daylight, and they badly needed to grab a little sleep.

"Yeah?"

"How many men have you killed?"

"Counting the War Between the States? Because, I'm not really sure about that, Laura. I have tried to just block what took place on the battlefields out of my mind."

"I understand. How many men have you had to kill as a United States marshal?"

"Quite a few."

She sat up and stared at him in the semidarkness. "More than five?"

"Uh-huh."

"More than a dozen?"

"Afraid so."

Laura's voice reflected her sadness. "Aren't you getting tired of all the killing?"

"I was tired of it after the first man that I dropped. The worst part for me isn't the bloodshed, it's the eyes."

"What do you mean?"

"I mean when you've shot a man his eyes are wild for a few moments and then they just flicker and die like a candle."

"I know. I've seen that as a nurse."

"The difference is that you have always tried to save lives . . . but I'm a lawman and so I've had to take lives. There's a world of difference in watching a person die when you are the cause of it."

"I don't understand how you can do that over and over."

"Someone has to do the job that I do. A preacher or a

priest might say that there are no really evil people . . . but I disagree. There are some men that are just no damn good. Never have been and never will be. And the sooner they are either hanged, shot, or imprisoned, the better."

"You might be right about that."

"Over the years I've given the subject plenty of thought. And I've come to the conclusion that if you study dogs, horses, and other animals, you quickly realize that some have it in their blood to fight and kill."

"But surely you don't think that humans are the same?"

"I'm afraid that I do, Laura. I've seen whole families where the parents were evil and all their children were going to be exactly the same way . . . even the daughters."

"Have you ever had to shoot a . . ."

He saw her hesitate and anticipated her next question. "You want to know if I've ever shot a woman? The answer is yes, but only in self-defense. And I have sent a few to the gallows."

"Did it bother you more to kill a woman than a man?"

"Why all these questions? I really don't want to think about killing now."

"But *did* it?"

"Yes. Killing a woman was harder on me than killing a man. Now, can we just go to sleep for an hour or so?"

"All right," she whispered. "But I really did need to know."

Longarm took some comfort in the fact that he had never shot a man down except in self-defense or when he couldn't make an arrest. And that knowledge allowed him to keep wearing a federal marshal's badge.

Laura reached out and took his hand. "You're a good man and a fine lover, Custis."

"Thank you."

"And I have all the faith in the world that everything is going to work out for the best."

"I hope so."

"I *know* so," she told him as he drifted off to sleep.

Chapter 13

Longarm and Laura rode out of Flagstaff about ten o'clock the next morning, on a cold and overcast day. The huge San Francisco Peaks were cloaked in wet, gray clouds, and they could hear the distant rumble of thunder.

"I'm glad we bought a couple of rain slickers," Longarm said as they followed a well-traveled road that roughly paralleled the Union Pacific rails westward toward California. "I think we're in for a downpour."

Laura nodded. She looked exhausted from the previous night's lovemaking and lack of sleep. Longarm hoped that they might find lodging for the night, even if it was in some rancher's barn. Anything to get out of a storm in this high country. He didn't expect that they would have to contend with snow, but at seven thousand feet, you could get it almost any time of the year.

"This is pretty country," she said, admiring the forest and meadows they were passing. "But I haven't seen even one river."

"Rivers are rare in Arizona. There are a few. The Gila,

the Salt, and the Verde, and of course the territory's north boundary is the Colorado River, which formed the Grand Canyon over millions of years."

"So how do the ranchers and towns get their water supply?"

"They dig deep wells and they have little lakes here and there. But water is precious up in this mountain country. That's why you don't see as many cattle here as in Colorado, Montana, or Wyoming."

"Do you think that we'll reach the Pittman Ranch before dark?"

"I don't know," Longarm replied. "But I expect we will. I'm thinking that it might be to our advantage to arrive about sunset. Supper will be on the table and everyone on the ranch will be gathered in one place, which is good."

"I sure hope this works out."

"You told me early this morning that you knew it would," Longarm reminded her. "Are you having second thoughts about coming along with me instead of going to the Grand Canyon?"

"Sure I am," she said a little irritably. "But I'm no quitter and I'm not fainthearted. I'll do my part."

"I've no doubt about that, Laura."

In the mid-afternoon, the storm broke and it began to rain hard. The wind picked up coming from the west straight into their faces. It was a cold, bone-chilling rain, and despite the slickers and their wide-brimmed hats, water found a way down under their shirts. Whenever Longarm glanced over at Laura, he could see her shivering, and her face was pale from both cold and fatigue.

"I see a little ranch up ahead and about a mile to the north," he told her as they topped a rise. "Maybe we can stop and rest for the evening and then get an early start in the morning."

"Perhaps it's the Pittman Ranch."

"It might be," Longarm agreed. "Although I don't see a sawmill nearby."

"It could be any place nearby in this thick ponderosa forest." Suddenly, she pointed. "Look! There's a wagon coming our way."

Longarm reined his horse off the road and into the cover of pines with Laura right behind him. The tall trees helped break the force of the wind and rain, and Longarm dismounted and helped Laura off her horse. She was so stiff and cold she had trouble standing.

"Who do you think it might be?" she asked.

"Could be anyone," he told her. "This is a heavily trafficked road."

"That's a huge wagon. Looks like it's stacked with lumber."

"If it is, then we're probably going to be meeting either a Pittman or someone who works for them." Longarm saw that the heavy wagon was being pulled by six powerful draft horses. "I'm going to get back on my horse and ride out to meet them. We need to know where the Pittman Ranch is located, and it could be the one that we just saw off to the north."

"What do you want me to do?"

"Stay hidden in these trees," Longarm answered. "If there is trouble, don't come out no matter what. Just stay in hiding."

Laura nodded, looking anxious. "Be careful!"

Longarm checked his pistol. He had also bought a good rifle in Flagstaff, but he didn't want to be holding it and therefore sending a signal to the driver and his companion that he was expecting trouble.

"I'll ask them where the ranch is," he said as he jammed his boot into the stirrup and swung up into the saddle. "This won't take long."

Minutes later he drew rein in the middle of the muddy road, pushed his rain slicker back from his gun, and forced himself to relax. If he was tense, that anxiety would be telegraphed to his horse and it might begin to fidget and dance. If the horse wasn't standing still and he had to fight with the animal, it would mean he'd have a tough time drawing his Colt and firing with any accuracy.

"Easy," he crooned to the animal. "Easy."

The lumber wagon wasn't moving very fast through the thick, red, and clinging mud that had already began to clog the road. Longarm saw that the driver and his companion both had their hats pulled low over their faces and that their horses were straining in their harness.

"Hello!" Longarm shouted into the pelting rain.

The two men on the wagon's seat snapped erect and looked so confused for a moment that Longarm wondered if they had both been dozing.

"Hold up there a minute!" Longarm called, reining his horse around the team and moving in closer to the driver.

"What the hell do you want?" the driver snapped.

"I want to know if that ranch just up ahead and a little to the north belongs to the Pittman family."

"Of course it does!"

"And do you work for them?"

The driver spat a thin stream of tobacco down into the mud and between the front legs of Longarm's mount. "Yep. You got any other stupid questions before we get along on our way?"

"Yeah," Longarm said. "Is Eli Pittman at the ranch?"

The driver and his companion visibly stiffened under their heavy canvas coats, and the driver asked, "Who wants to know?"

"An old friend."

They stared down at him, and the second man said, "Maybe you're no friend at all. Maybe you're the United States marshal that Elias told us about and you're after Eli."

Longarm smiled up into the rain. "You must be a real smart fella to have guessed that, because I *am* the marshal that kicked the shit out of Elias and means to do a whole lot more to Eli."

The driver tried to tunnel his hand under his big coat, and it didn't take a mind reader to know that he and his companion were going for their guns. Longarm had them beat by a mile, and when he pointed his big pistol up at them, the pair froze.

"Don't kill us!" the one beside the driver cried. "We didn't do nothin' wrong!"

"Set the brake and both of you climb down from that wagon."

When Longarm had them grounded, he dismounted and then disarmed the pair.

"What are you gonna do to us?" the driver demanded, trying to sound angry, but instead showing his fear.

"I haven't decided just yet," Longarm told the men. "But if you do as I say, you both just might get through this alive. Take off your coats and hats."

"What! In this weather!"

"The wind and rain won't kill you," Longarm said, "but I might."

The driver exploded. "Son of a bitch! We don't deserve to be treated this way!"

"It's a hard and cruel world," Longarm said without a hint of sympathy. "But if you step lively, you'll stay warm enough on the hike into Flagstaff."

"You're expecting us to walk all the way to Flagstaff!" the driver protested. "In this damn storm?"

"Get moving."

"Well what are we supposed to do when we get to Flagstaff?"

"How the hell would I know?" Longarm answered. "Now, move!"

"But this is Mr. Pittman's wagon and team of horses! We have a delivery to make in town. That lumber is expected to . . ."

"Move!" Longarm shouted, pointing at them and waving his gun.

The two freighters turned their backs on Longarm and started walking. Over the rumble of distant thunder, he could hear them both furiously cussing him.

"All right!" Longarm called out to Laura still hidden in the pines. "You can ride out now."

Seconds later, Laura came trotting out to the road. "Why did you make them give up the wagon and then send the poor men off without their coats in this cold rain?"

"We're going to put those coats on and drive this wagon right into the Pittman Ranch yard," Longarm told her. "And when they look out their window and see the wagon with all this lumber coming back home, they'll rush outside to find out what the hell is going on."

"And that's when you hope to get the drop on them," Laura said.

"That's right. But there is one thing that worries me about this plan."

"And what would that be?"

"If Eli or Elias rushes out and is armed, he might go for his gun. And if one of 'em does that, you'll be sitting right up on the wagon beside me."

"Oh my gosh," she said as the full impact of his words struck her. "What . . ."

Longarm reached up and touched her leg. "We'll only have a few seconds before they realize we aren't their drivers. I'll have my pistol out, but sometimes if men are surprised and maybe they've been drinking or are just downright stupid, they'll go for their guns. If they do, you have to promise me you'll jump off the wagon on the off side and run like hell."

Laura thought about that for a moment before saying, "I'd rather die fighting than running. If they manage to kill you . . . a federal marshal . . . what chance do you think I'd have as a witness?"

"You're right. They'd have to kill you as well."

"So the question is, do you want me to have the rifle or your pistol?"

Longarm shook his head, thinking maybe this wasn't such a good idea after all. The last thing he wanted was to have Laura shot.

"I'm going with you," she said, dismounting to grab the smaller of the coats and hats. "So which weapon do you want me to have close at hand?"

"The rifle," Longarm told her. "I like my chances better with my Colt."

"Then grab the other coat and hat and let's get this over with," she told him. "I'm soaked to the bone and freezing cold, and I sure don't plan to camp out in the rain tonight under these pines."

"Okay," he said, face grim with determination. "Let's tie our horses to the back of this lumber wagon where they won't be seen as we approach the ranch house, and we'll let the cards fall where they may."

"I hope that there is a good hot supper on the fire and they haven't drunk all the whiskey."

"Me too," Longarm said as he shrugged out of his rain slicker, squeezed into a coat that was much too small, and then replaced his flat-brimmed hat with a battered and dirty Stetson.

When the horses were tied behind the wagon, Longarm released the brake and turned the big lumber wagon around. The time for talking and planning was past. Now it was time to get in out of the storm, either dead . . . or alive.

Chapter 14

They left the main road and followed a dirt track toward the ranch house. When they were still a hundred yards from the log cabin, the front door flew open and five men piled out into the rain to stare at them.

"Dammit," Longarm muttered. "I was hoping they wouldn't see this wagon coming back so soon."

"So what do we do now?" Laura asked.

"Only thing we can do is stick to our plan. Just keep your hat down low and your hands near that rifle."

"I don't like this at all."

"If you want me to stop this wagon, I'll do it. You could walk back to our saddle horses, mount up, and ride like hell back to Flagstaff."

Laura thought about that a moment before she shook her head. "No. I'm sticking right beside you. At least none of them are holding rifles."

"No," Longarm said as they moved ever closer. "They still just think we're their drivers and that there must be some problem with the wagon or maybe one of the draft horses. Right now, they're just curious. But pretty damn quick curious is going to turn to fightin' mad."

When they entered the ranch yard, Elias Pittman detached from the others and yelled, "What the hell is goin' on, Jake? Why are you comin' back?"

Longarm felt Laura shift nervously beside him on the seat. "Steady," he whispered. "Just be still and keep quiet."

"Hey!" Elias hollered, marching forward. "Gawdamnit, why the hell did you turn that wagon around?"

Longarm raised his left hand in a silent greeting. He wanted to get to within fifty feet of the men before he whipped out his Colt and had them empty-handed.

Elias was cussing, and the other four men moved forward behind him. Longarm pulled on the lines, set the brake on the big lumber wagon, and reached across his belt buckle to grab his pistol. He drew it out from under his coat, cocked back the hammer, and said, "Surprise, Elias! It's United States Marshal Custis Long and I'd like you to slowly raise your hands just like you're praisin' the Lord."

Elias blinked, and then he did a stupid thing. He went for his gun, only it was under his raincoat, and the hammer got caught up in the slicker, and he lost a few precious seconds as he struggled.

Longarm shot the man in his right thigh. Elias bellowed and staggered, then finally tore his gun free, raised it, and died with a bullet ripping through his forehead. He flopped over backward into the mud.

The other four men jumped for the door to the ranch house and slammed it behind them, while Longarm sent a few bullets into the cabin just to make sure they understood that they would get the same thing Elias had gotten if they chose to be foolish.

Laura stammered, "He's dead!"

"Deader than a doornail," Longarm replied. "He was twice stupid on me and there was no help for it."

"But . . ."

"Grab the rifle and get behind the wagon!"

Suddenly, the glass panes in the front windows exploded outward, and Longarm saw guns and rifles coming to bear on them. He shoved Laura, and they tumbled off the wagon, landing in the mud with a smacking sound.

"Behind the wagon!" he shouted. "Untie our horses!"

A wild volley of gunfire erupted from the ranch house as Longarm and Laura crabbed through the clinging red mud. He could hear wood splintering as bullets tore into the wagon. The terrified team of horses were jumping and lunging, and even given the immense weight of the wagon and despite the fact that its brake was set, everything began to slide across the ranch yard.

Longarm was behind cover, and before the powerful draft horses moved much farther, he grabbed Laura and propelled her toward their saddle horses. He quickly untied them and dragged their rifle out of the mud, gave it to her after she was mounted, and yelled, "Try to keep the wagon between you and the ranch house! Go!"

Laura gave him a wide-eyed glance and booted her horse into a hard gallop back up the road. Her gelding's hooves cupped the mud and slung it up at the leaden sky. Longarm holstered his Colt revolver, swung up into the saddle, and beat a hasty retreat after the woman. The

Pittman cowboys were filling the air with bullets, but he knew that they didn't have a clear shot and that the visibility was poor.

When they reached the main road, Laura drew up her horse and waited anxiously. "Dammit, Custis, what is your next brilliant idea? That didn't work out well at all and a man just died!"

"Elias had a simple choice and he made the wrong one," Longarm said, drawing his horse up to a sliding stop in the thick mud.

"But we don't even know if Eli was there or not!"

"Sure we do," Longarm said, putting his horse to a trot and pulling the flat brim of his hat down lower over his eyes. "If Eli Pittman was at the ranch, he would have been the one out front who had died. Or maybe I'd have died because Eli is one helluva lot smarter and quicker with a gun than his brother."

"So that's it?"

"Yep."

Laura drove her horse up to trot along beside him. She had lost her hat and she was covered from head to toe with mud. Longarm glanced sideways at her, and had he not known she was a beautiful woman, he would have thought she was some beaten saloon brawler who had just been kicked around in the mud.

"What else is there?" he asked. "We had to learn if Eli was there or not and we did."

"At the expense of a man's *life*?"

"He was no damn good. Elias was a pigheaded fool. and I wouldn't be a bit surprised if he had already killed a few good men. If you want to mourn the man's passing, please do it in silence."

"But . . . but I can't stand this cold and mud and rain!"

"Then let's find shelter," he told her. "But first we'd better cover a few miles. You never know if those other four might get some whiskey courage and decide to follow our tracks."

"Oh, shit," she said in frustration or futility. "I can't believe what just happened back there."

"Believe it," Longarm said. "And if you can't stand the heat, then you had damn sure better get away from the fire."

"And *you're* the fire."

"That's right," Longarm told her. "Eli Pittman double-crossed me and my boss when he tried to kill us back in Denver. And if you think that I'm soon gonna be forgettin' that, then you'd better rethink everything and get away from me just as far and as fast as you can, because someone else is going to die before much longer."

Laura hung her head and rode along beside him for another mile before she said, "You're a judge, jury, and executioner all rolled into one body, Custis. You are a badge-wearing killer while I'm a healer."

Longarm could hear resignation and maybe something else in her voice, and he replied, "So tell me something that we both didn't already know. And while you're at it, tell me what I could have done differently and still learned if Eli was in that ranch house or not."

But Laura couldn't think of anything to tell the big deputy United States marshal, so she rode along through the cold falling rain just hoping they would come upon a ranch house, a farm, or even an abandoned barn so they could get out of the downpour and maybe even get dry and warm.

* * *

Two long and miserable hours later they finally saw the lights of a farmhouse in the distance. It was nearly dark, and both Longarm and Laura were shivering uncontrollably from cold and fatigue. Their horses weren't doing a whole lot better, because it had been tough going through the clinging mud of this high mountain road.

"We'll spend the night here," he said, pointing toward the cabin.

Laura managed to shake her head. "Maybe they won't even take us in, given the way we look."

"They'll take us in one way or the other," Longarm assured her. "And I'll pay them for their food, shelter, and trouble. But just one thing you have to remember."

"What?"

"Don't tell them that I just killed Elias Pittman. They'd only be alarmed, and that would make things all the more difficult for everyone."

"If the Pittman family learns that they helped us, I'm pretty sure that whoever lives at that farmhouse would have good reason to be more than a little alarmed."

"That's true, but we'll deal with it tomorrow," Longarm told her. "Just let me do all the talking."

"Of course," she said through chattering teeth.

When they slogged up to the cabin, Longarm reined his horse in and shouted, "Hello the house!"

There was a little porch, and the door under it opened slowly to reveal a short, white-bearded man with a shotgun clenched in his hands. "Both of you keep your hands in plain sight!"

They raised their hands and Longarm said, "I'm a

federal officer of the law and this is my lady friend. We are cold, wet, and hungry, and we need food for us and these horses, along with shelter. Can you help us?"

"Can you pay for what you need?"

"I can," Longarm said. "And I will."

"I'll see your badge right now."

Longarm was careful to reach slowly into his pocket and show the man his federal officer's badge.

"Looks real," the short man said, lowering his shotgun. "Put the horses in the barn, wash off all that mud in the horse trough, and come inside. I got pork and beans on the stove and some whiskey to warm your innards."

"Thank you," Laura whispered.

"Are you *really* a woman?" the short man asked. "What you doin' out in this storm with a lawman?"

"It's a long story," she said. "No pun intended."

"Huh?"

"I'll explain it all to you after we get inside."

The man dipped his chin with understanding. "My name is Gabe Wilson. I got a wife and a boy inside, and they're mighty nervous about your showin' up lookin' like you are on such a mean evenin'."

"Understandable," Longarm said, wearily dismounting and then helping Laura to do the same.

"There's hay and some oats in the barn. Put your horses up with the calves and they'll be fine for the night."

"I'll do it," Longarm promised as he took the reins from Laura's cold, muddy hand. To her he said, "You go on inside and get cleaned up as best that you can. I'll be along."

Laura stumbled up on the porch, swaying with weariness. "Mr. Wilson, where is the horse trough I'm supposed to wash up in?"

"Never mind that," the man said. "You bein' a woman, my missus will take proper care of you."

"I could use a shot of your whiskey right off, Mr. Wilson."

"Well I expect that you could," he said as he stepped aside and let Laura pass into the cabin.

Longarm headed for the barn, leading the two horses. He was beyond being tired, and he was concerned that the Pittman gang would be coming after them. But probably not tonight and not in this storm . . . if ever. They'd have a dead fool to bury, and while they might be bent on vengeance, they would remember what a big federal marshal had done and they would be justifiably afraid.

Chapter 15

"So," Laura asked the next afternoon as they rode through the little town of Ash Fork and headed south toward Arizona's territorial capital, "did you tell Mr. Wilson about the shoot-out we had at the Pittman Ranch?"

"Not in so many words," Longarm replied vaguely.

"What *did* you tell the man? I mean, he really needs to know that you killed Elias."

"I think the less that family knows about the shoot-out the better off they will be," Longarm told her. "We left in the rain this morning, so I'm pretty sure that our tracks to the Wilson cabin won't be evident. There is no reason for that family to be involved, and they certainly wouldn't have much of a chance against a vengeful Pittman bunch."

The rain had stopped for the last several hours, but the sky was overcast and the day was cold and windy. "I suppose that's true," Laura said. "They were a very nice family. I had the feeling that things were pretty hard for them."

"I had the same impression and left them three dollars. But the truth is that they're living in country too high to give them much of a growing season," Longarm told her. "Mr. Wilson had come to that same conclusion and said that they were going to start raising more sheep. Summer a flock up there in the mountains and then winter them down around Ash Fork where the elevation is lower and the winters are much milder."

"How much farther is it to Prescott?" she asked. "I'm sure tired of riding in this bad weather."

"If we push hard, we'll be there before dark," Longarm promised. "And to be honest, I'm not much happier about the weather than you are."

"Maybe we should have sold these horses and taken the stagecoach out of Ash Fork."

"Maybe." Longarm watched a golden eagle soar out of the thick stands of piñon and juniper pine. "But having a horse gives me the alternative of going after Eli Pittman if I spook him and he decides to run."

"Is Arizona's capital quite large?"

"No. If I remember correctly, there's a small army fort that has pretty much been abandoned since the Indians quit raiding. The capitol building itself is built of granite and is quite impressive. It stands in the middle of a square of businesses and what is called Whiskey Row. Prescott is a nice place to visit. Not too hot in the summer or cold in the winter."

"Maybe I'll like it better even than Flagstaff."

"What about that handsome and charming newspaper editor you met a few days ago?"

Laura smiled. "I want a man who will go where I go . . . not the other way around."

"You're a real ballbuster."

Her eyebrows arched in surprise. "A *what*?"

"Never mind," Longarm said. "Let's push these horses a little harder. I have a feeling that another storm is heading our way and I'd like to beat it to Prescott."

"Amen!" Laura said as they forced their tired mounts into a gallop.

They arrived at the outskirts of the territorial capital an hour before sundown, and a big and professionally hand-painted sign told them:

TERRITORIAL GOVERNOR PATRICK WOODRUFF
WELCOMES YOU TO PRESCOTT, ARIZONA,
FIRST SETTLED IN 1864 BY MINERS PROSPECTING
FOR GOLD. PRESCOTT WAS SELECTED BY
PRESIDENT ABRAHAM LINCOLN TO BECOME
ARIZONA'S FIRST TERRITORIAL GOVERNMENT. IN 1867,
THE SKUNKS DOWN IN TUCSON TOOK AWAY OUR
CAPITOL BUT WE RIGHTFULLY GOT IT BACK IN 1877.
POPULATION 3,028 ELEVATION 5,5346.

Longarm shook his head. "It sounds like there's been a lot of politicking going on in this Arizona Territory, which is pretty typical out in the West. The way I heard it, Tucson was a hotbed of Southern sympathizers and everyone thought that Arizona was going to be a bonanza with its gold, silver, and copper. Copper is big here, but the huge gold field that influenced the Civil War and helped finance it for the Union was the Comstock Lode in Nevada."

"I don't want a history lesson," Laura grumped as the first scattering of raindrops began to fall. "Let's find a stable, then a hotel, and get out of this coming storm!"

"Yes, ma'am," Longarm replied as he pushed his horse down busy Gurley Street.

For appearance' sake, they took separate rooms at the Hotel St. Michael, which was a fine three-story brick building located directly across from the Courthouse Plaza. After hot baths and a change into clean, dry clothes, they dined in the hotel's lobby and enjoyed the usual libations. As was his practice, Longarm sat with his back to a wall and watched everyone who came and went through the lobby.

"You never know if Eli Pittman and his wife might just suddenly appear."

"That would be quite the coincidence," Laura said. "This is a pretty big and bustling town."

"Yes," he agreed. "And tomorrow we will start out asking questions at the saloons, liveries, and newspaper office just like we did in Flagstaff. I'm sure by the time we meet up for lunch, we'll have learned about all that we need to know concerning Eli, his wife, and the governor, who I'm guessing has recovered from his wounds."

"Maybe he died," Laura suggested.

Longarm signaled the waiter. "Excuse me," he said. "We've just arrived here and we had heard a rumor that your governor was shot not long ago."

"That's right," the man said, leaning in closer. "But it wasn't really too serious. Oh, Governor Woodruff had his people spread the rumor that he was fighting for his life, but what was later learned is that a drunken miner who had a grudge against the governor shot him in the ass."

"In the *ass*?" Longarm questioned.

"Yes." The waiter smiled and turned to Laura. "Excuse me, miss. I should have said 'buttocks' in your presence. But the truth of it is that the wound was superficial and went through both of the man's butt cheeks. Our governor is rather... rotund and he had a lot of extra padding to absorb the bullet."

"So he was only wounded by some drunk who was mad at him?" Longarm asked.

"That's right. The miner was sentenced to a month in the town's jail and fined a hundred dollars." The waiter winked. "As you can well imagine, there was a lot of joking going on about the shooting incident. About half the town said that they wished the miner had been a better shot, and hats were passed around in the saloons. Not only was a hundred dollars raised to pay the man's court fine ... but there was plenty enough left over to make him a fine silver medal for exemplary service!"

They all laughed and Longarm said, "I seem to recall that there was a man named Eli Pittman who married a woman named Rachel and that they were related to the governor."

"Well sure she is! Mrs. Rachel Pittman is not someone that a man could easily forget. Oh, she's not as pretty as you, ma'am. But she's a looker and she just seems to draw a man's attention."

"I understand," Longarm said. "Are they in town right now?"

"Mr. and Mrs. Pittman?"

"Yes."

The waiter's smile faded. "Why are you askin' so many questions about that pair, if I may be so bold as to inquire?"

"I've met Eli Pittman and thought I'd renew our acquaintance," Longarm said, trying to sound very casual. "Any idea where I might find him?"

"I'm afraid not," the waiter said before hurrying away.

When they were alone again, Longarm frowned. "Did you see how quickly that man's whole demeanor changed when I began to ask about Eli?"

"Yes," Laura replied. "He went from jovial to icy in about two seconds. Why was that, do you suppose?"

"I have no idea." Longarm finished his brandy and stifled a yawn. "We need to get some sleep. Tomorrow is going to be a long and very interesting day."

She arched an eyebrow upward. "Does that mean that you aren't coming to visit my room tonight?"

"I sleepwalk and I just might find your room."

"Knock three times and I'll let you in."

They both grinned before Longarm paid their bill and they headed up to their rooms.

Chapter 16

Longarm and Laura had a quiet breakfast and then left the hotel at ten o'clock to canvass the town for information. Before they parted, Longarm described Eli Pittman and added a warning: "If you see the man, try not to attract his attention. Just note where he is going and then come looking for me."

"And if you see him on the streets this morning?"

Longarm didn't hesitate to reply. "If I see Eli and he sees me, lead is going to fly, and when the gunsmoke clears only one of us will be left standing."

"Then I hope that I see him before you do," Laura said as she exited the hotel.

After their separation, Longarm decided that the first stop he needed to make was at the local marshal's office as a professional courtesy. It was easy to find, and when he entered the small building, he saw that there were two lawmen drinking coffee and sitting at their desk smoking cigarettes. The man that he assumed was the town marshal was in his early fifties, fat and mild-looking, with a vest and the rosy cheeks of a man who liked to drink to excess. The younger man was about thirty, tall, slender, and much better dressed. He had on expensive boots and a silk shirt, and his gun had a pearl handle that Longarm doubted was bought with the wages of an ordinary deputy. Neither of the men bothered to come out of his chair when Longarm entered, but instead they just stared at him without even a nod in greeting.

"Good morning," Longarm said before introducing himself and stating the nature of his business in coming to Prescott.

When he was finished, the older man with the rosy face and washed-out blue eyes said, "I'm Marshal Andy Hagan and this is my deputy, Joe Cotter. Would you like some coffee? It's pretty strong, stale, and we don't have any sugar, but it gives you a lift on a morning."

"I drink it straight black and I'd appreciate a cup," Longarm replied, deciding that it might make this meeting go smoother.

"Marshal Long, go ahead and pull up a chair," Hagan offered as he motioned for his deputy to pour Longarm a cup. "When did you arrive in my town?"

"Last evening. I'd have come here right away, but it was starting to rain again and we were tired."

"'We'?"

Longarm silently cussed himself for his revealing slip of the tongue. "I came with a lady from Denver."

Both of the Prescott lawmen grinned, and Deputy Cotter said, "You federal people sure do travel in style. Why, how nice it must be to have a woman to hump while you're on the road."

Longarm's smile died. "I think you'd better keep your tongue and mind civil, Deputy Cotter. I don't appreciate your loose talk."

Cotter's mocking smile froze on his lean face. "And I don't much care for you federal people coming here to mess around with our town."

"Hold on, you two," Marshal Hagan said, shaking a hand at them. "Let's just keep things civil here."

"I'd like that," Longarm said, "but I can see that your young deputy has a nasty streak and a dirty mind. I think you need to school him in professional manners."

"Screw you!" Cotter hissed.

Longarm was about to say something to the deputy, when his boss said, "Listen, Marshal Long, the truth of it is that what you've told us about Eli Pittman just doesn't fit with what we know about the man."

"Then you don't know him very well," Longarm snapped.

"Maybe that is true," Hagan said, "but I *do* know that you have just brought me some serious trouble."

"And why is that?" Longarm asked, blowing steam off his coffee and leaning back in a chair that felt like it was about to collapse.

"Well," Hagan said, eyeing Longarm closely, "for one thing Eli Pittman is related by marriage to our territorial governor."

"So I've heard. Longarm sipped his coffee, which was just awful. He sat his cup down on the scarred desk. "But connected or not, the man attempted to murder myself and my boss, United States Marshal Billy Vail."

"Any chance that it might have been someone else?" Hagan asked hopefully.

"No chance at all."

Hagan shook his head. "Well now we really have ourselves a situation, don't we?"

"I don't understand the problem," Longarm said, feeling irritation. "Eli Pittman is wanted for attempted murder. I've come all the way from Denver to find and arrest him. If he cooperates and I don't have to kill Eli, then I'll haul his ass back to Denver, where he will stand trial. There is no doubt that he will be found guilty and sentenced to a long prison term." Longarm glanced from the marshal to his deputy. "So what is complicated or difficult about what I've just told you?"

"Well, let me enlighten you, Marshal Long. The fact is that Eli Pittman was just appointed by Governor Woodruff to the Arizona Rangers. And not just as a regular Ranger, but as a *captain* in the Rangers."

"Is Captain Pittman in your town?"

"Nope," Hagan said, looking pleased. "He left two days ago to join the Arizona Rangers on some assignment."

"Assignment to *where*?" Longarm asked.

"Hell if I know," Marshal Hagan replied. "You see, the Arizona Rangers are an elite but somewhat loosely organized bunch that operates under Governor Woodruff's direction. They often go south to fight Mexican cattle rustlers and slave traders as well as the renegade Apache. It's a wild and a mostly lawless area down there along the border and the invaders from Mexico sometimes have to be punished."

Longarm scowled. "So you're telling me that Eli Pittman might even be in Mexico?"

"That's right." Marshal Hagan took a sip of the terrible

coffee then blew another smoke ring at his fly-specked ceiling. "And furthermore, I don't think that you even have the authority to arrest Captain Pittman."

Longarm almost jumped out of his rickety office chair. "What the hell makes you think that!"

"Do you have any legal paperwork or a judge's arrest warrant?" Marshal Hagan asked.

"No."

Hagan sighed as if he were already weary of this conversation. "Hmmm . . . then you have nothing to back up your story that Captain Pittman actually was the shooter?"

"Dammit, I saw him!" Longarm growled. "He and I stood face-to-face in my hotel room and I barely escaped with my life. Same for my boss, Marshal Vail."

"But you have no paperwork? Just *your* word against that of Captain Pittman?" Hagan questioned, making it clear that Pittman's word would be held highest in the Arizona Territory.

Longarm stared at the smug-looking Prescott lawman and then thought he detected a sneer on the younger lawman's face. "Now, wait just a minute!" he said, voice rising. "I came one hell of a long way to get here, and I'm not leaving this territory without either killing Eli or arresting him."

Hagan's face changed and his voice grew nasty. "Let me tell you something, Marshal Long. In *my* town and in this territory we don't much care for the federal government or the people that they send to meddle in our affairs. So my suggestion would be to get your ass back to Denver and explain to your boss and any other federal bureaucrat that we don't give a tinker's damn about your business."

Longarm slammed his coffee cup down so hard on the desk that it erupted in a geyser across the desktop and strewn papers. "If you oppose me on this, Marshal Hagan, you'll come to regret that fact."

"Are you threatening me and my deputy?" the man asked.

"I'm just giving you a piece of good, professional advice. One lawman to another. Take it or leave it, but either way I'm going to find and get my man before I leave this territory."

"Oh," Deputy Cotter said, huffing with derision, "you are a cocky one but you sure ain't got any idea what you are up against."

"Yes, I do," Longarm said, rising from his chair. "I've just realized that I'm not only up against Eli, but you two as well. So now that we've all had our little say and laid our cards out on the table, I think I'll go about my business without your help or interference."

"You are a long way from Denver," Cotter told him. "You ought to just get out of Prescott while you can. And by the way, this woman that you're traveling with . . . is she any good in bed?"

Longarm grabbed his cup of coffee and hurled what was left of the hot liquid at the deputy's face, but Cotter was quick and ducked most of the coffee. "Damn you!" he shouted, stepping forward.

Longarm came forward as well, and he buried his fist into Deputy Cotter's midsection. The man folded up and Longarm belted him in the ear. Cotter went down wailing in pain. Longarm didn't see Marshal Hagan leave his chair, and he didn't see the gun butt that came arching toward the back of his head. All he saw was a flash of bright stars as he lost consciousness and hit the tobacco-stained and dirty wooden floor.

Chapter 17

"So what are you going to do with him?" Deputy Joe Cotter asked, gazing down at the unconscious federal marshal. "Andy, I swear that if it was up to me, I'd . . ."

"Well, it *ain't* up to you," Marshal Hagan snapped. "The last thing I needed was for that big son of a bitch to show up and cause me or Governor Woodruff trouble. You know that your uncle is expecting to serve another term, and this situation with Pittman could prove to become a real political boondoggle."

Deputy Cotter looked down at his shirt and cussed at the fresh coffee stains. His head was ringing from the blow that he'd received at the hands of the now unconscious federal marshal, and he felt dizzy and enraged.

"That big bastard tried to scald and then kill me, Andy!"

"I know. I saw it, but you sure provoked him with that talk about his woman," the marshal said. "Let's disarm this one and drag his ass into a cell."

"Then what will we do?"

"You go home and get cleaned up and I'll stay here until you get back," Marshal Hagan decided. "Then I'm going to go see Governor Woodruff this morning and fill him in on this damned mess. He can decide what our next move will be."

"I hope he tells us to kill Marshal Long and that would make the whole problem go away."

"Well, I can promise you that he won't tell us to do that. Governor Woodruff wouldn't dare order such a thing."

"Don't be too sure about that," Cotter said. "Getting reappointed for another term is about the most important thing in my uncle's life."

"Doing away with this federal marshal is just too risky at this time," Marshal Hagan said. "We'll have to deal with it some other way, and that's exactly what the governor and I will be talking about while you watch over our new prisoner."

"Maybe he'll make an attempt to escape and I'll have no choice but to shoot him," Deputy Cotter suggested with a tight grin. "You or the governor wouldn't have to have any part of that. It would just be an unfortunate incident between Federal Marshal Long and me."

"Don't even think about it."

Cotter couldn't hide his disappointment. "Maybe you're right," he finally said. "I guess the easiest thing would be for us to let that big bastard loose so he can go chasing Captain Pittman down toward the border with Mexico. Pittman and his hardscrabble Rangers will handle the problem once and for all."

"Not a bad idea," Marshal Hagan said. "It's the solution that I'll suggest to Governor Woodruff this morning."

Later that morning, Marshal Hagan arrived at the capitol building and requested a special meeting with the governor, making sure that the governor's secretary understood that it was very important to see the man at once.

Ten minutes later, he was ushered into the governor's opulent office and the door was closed behind him for privacy. Governor Patrick Woodruff was a handsome man in his early sixties, of average height but with a thick shock of silver hair and a strong chin with a goatee. He had been a general in the Union Army and he was known to be as decisive as he was bold and opinionated. Governor Woodruff walked with a limp and a cane, but he considered both to be a political asset because they reminded people of his battlefield bravery at Bull Run.

"Ah," the governor said, clasping his hands together as he leaned over his desk. "What is so serious that it would make you insist on seeing me this morning? I have several meetings, so this has to be brief."

Marshal Hagan liked and respected the governor. He and his wife were always invited to the Governor's Christmas Ball and other important social events, and he knew that Governor Woodruff would always support him and even promote his career given a fair opportunity.

"Well, Governor, we have a little problem that we have deal with right away."

"Sit down and get to the point, Andy."

Marshal Hagan took a seat in front of the governor's splendid desk and laid out the problem as clearly and concisely as he could, and ended by saying, "As you know, Eli was appointed as a captain of the Arizona Rangers by you less than a week ago. Also, being related to Rachel and . . ."

"Stop!" Governor Woodruff ordered, reaching into a silver box for a bit of snuff. "Let me think a minute here. This is really quite disturbing. Do you believe this Marshal Custis Long and the charges of attempted murder against Eli?"

"I'm afraid that I do," Hagan said. "We both know that Eli has a very dark and violent side to him."

"Yes, I have always known. That was the primary reason why I gave him the appointment in the Rangers."

"You mean you were hoping that he would . . ."

"Don't say it," Governor Woodruff snapped. "But yes, I was thinking that Eli might conveniently die a gallant death in the line of duty, and that would have taken care of a long-standing thorn in my side as well as freeing Rachel of the worst mistake in her young, turbulent life. It would have been perfect, and now we have this federal marshal problem."

"Marshal Long has no paperwork. No proof at this time other than his word that Eli tried to kill him and his superior back in Denver."

"Ah, but the marshal *could* get proof if necessary. It might take a bit of time to get it from Denver, but I have no doubt it is available, and the resulting arrest warrant from a federal judge would tie my hands and give me no choice but to go public about these charges."

"Right before you apply for your next reappointment."

"Exactly." The governor's fists balled in anger and frustration. "I love Rachel, but sometimes she drives me almost to drink. I told her . . . pleaded with her . . . not to marry Eli Pittman, but would she listen? No! Now look what we have staring us all in the face."

"I do have a possible solution," Marshal Hagan offered, dangling hope like a worm on a fish hook.

The governor looked up suddenly. "Then let's hear it."

Marshal Hagan took credit for the idea even though he knew he should have admitted it was to his deputy's credit. "And so," he ended up saying, "I release this man from my jail and tell him where to find Captain Pittman and we let him be killed down by the border."

"But what if this Marshal Long should kill Eli first?" the governor asked. "I'm sure that he is not without his own fighting skills."

"I agree," Hagan said. "Custis Long strikes me as a very tough man, and I'm sure he is no slouch with a pistol or rifle."

"Then . . ."

"Governor," Hagan interrupted. "What we would have to do is to warn Captain Pittman that this federal marshal was coming to arrest him for attempted murder. Once he was warned, I've not a doubt in my mind that the matter would be taken care of . . . permanently . . . and with no bad publicity or political damage to your reputation."

Governor Woodruff nodded his fine, shaggy head in solemn agreement. "Yes," he said at last. "Captain Pittman, backed by those tough Arizona Rangers, would certainly make short work of the federal marshal."

"Problem solved!" Hagan exclaimed. "And we have kept our hands completely clean in the matter."

"Who can be sent south to warn Captain Pittman and

perhaps even to make sure that he along with Marshal Long never return to Prescott or are heard from again?"

"Only one man that I know of is capable of the assignment," Hagan said quietly.

"You?"

"No," Hagan confessed. "I'm too old and fat to handle this job. I would recommend my deputy and your nephew, Deputy Cotter."

The governor's eyes widened for a moment. "Are you sure that he is up this?"

"I'm as sure he could do it as I'm sure that the sun will rise tomorrow morning."

"Then send Joe at once to warn Captain Pittman."

"I'll do that, but he'll want something in return."

The governor nodded. "Money."

"Money and some kind of political appointment that would give him far more status than he has as my lowly deputy."

"I can think of something later," Governor Woodruff said. "Just get Joe on the trail south at once."

"And the marshal I'm holding in a jail cell?"

"Find a reason to keep him jailed for at least two days to give my nephew a good head start."

"I'll do that," Marshal Hagan promised.

"Good!" The territorial governor rose to his feet and expressed both relief and confidence. "You are doing a *fine* job, Andy. Keep up the outstanding work and good things will definitely come your way."

"I'm counting on that, Governor."

The two men shook hands, and then Marshal Andy Hagan hurried off to take care of this new and very important business.

Chapter 18

"Dammit, Hagan, let me out of here!" Longarm shouted. "I'm a federal officer of the law and you're gonna catch hell for this!"

Prescott's Marshal Hagan yawned and rolled another cigarette. He leaned far back in his office chair, and when he was satisfied with his smoke, he pulled a match from his drawer, scratched it across the surface of the old desk, and inhaled deeply. "Shouts and threats won't get you freed one minute sooner, Marshal Long."

"I've got a man to catch!"

"You've also got a judge to see," Hagan reminded him. "And I'm afraid that Judge Klein is a bit under the weather these days. As soon as he's able to get out of his sickbed and into the courtroom, I promise you'll be brought before him for sentencing."

"Sentencing!" Longarm roared. "For what?"

"For attacking my deputy, of course. You did a lot of damage to poor Joe, and he hadn't raised a finger you."

"He insulted Miss Danby. You heard him."

"I heard my deputy make a remark about the woman that was probably not in good taste," Hagan admitted. "But that sure didn't warrant knocking the shit out of Joe Cotter."

Longarm paced back and forth in his cell and then stopped and said, "Did you send someone over to the Hotel St. Michael to tell Miss Danby that I'm being held behind bars?"

"Not yet. You see, thanks to the whipping you gave him, Deputy Cotter isn't available, and I need to stay here and watch over you. It's my sworn duty, Marshal Long. All of this trouble falls directly on *your* head, not mine."

"Dammit! You are really rubbing my fur the wrong way."

"Well," Hagan said, blowing a lazy smoke ring, "if you hadn't attacked my deputy, you wouldn't be in this situation."

Longarm tromped over to his bed, which was a thin straw mattress, and flopped down on it, to stare up at the ceiling. "You know what I think?" he asked to the ceiling as his head continued to radiate pain.

"Nope," Hagan replied. "And I really don't care."

"I think you are trying to keep me in here in order to help Eli Pittman. That's what you're doing."

"You can think whatever you like, but until Judge Klein is well enough to sentence you for attacking a local lawman, you'll stay locked up."

Longarm was so mad that he could almost have bitten through the iron bars of his miserable little cell. But being angry wasn't going to do him any damn good, so he forced his mind to calm down. He was certain that Marshal Hagen was playing a game on him in order to buy time for Eli, but whatever he was thinking was of no good use until he was set free.

Longarm must have drifted off to sleep, because he was suddenly awakened by Laura's angry shouting. "You can't lock up a United States marshal and keep him behind bars!"

"I beg to disagree with you on that one," Hagan told her. "Because, as you can plainly see, I *have* arrested your friend from Denver and he *is* locked behind my bars. And that is where he is going to remain until Judge Klein is able to hear his case."

"This is ridiculous!" Laura stormed about, marching around the man and coming over to Longarm's cell. "Custis, what happened?"

Longarm touched the back of his head and felt the dried and matted blood in his hair. "I lost my temper and hit his dammed dirty-mouthed deputy and then Marshal Hagen hit me over the head with a pistol from behind."

Laura frowned. "Why did you attack his deputy?"

"Never you mind," Longarm replied, not wanting to tell Laura that he had been defending her honor. "Just help me get out of here by finding the judge and telling him that I need to arrest Eli Pittman."

"*Captain* Pittman," Hagan corrected. "And as we told you before, the captain is down along the Mexican border riding with the Arizona Rangers. He might be back next week, or he might be back next month. You can never tell because his work is very dangerous."

"Go find Judge Klein and plead with him to write a

note or something so that I can be released," Longarm told Laura. "I need to get out of here in a hurry."

"I'll do that right now," Laura promised, squeezing his hand through the bars. "Do you also need to see a doctor for that cut on the back of your poor head?"

"I probably could have used a few stitches earlier, but now I'm fine," Longarm told her. "Just get me released."

"I will." She turned and hurried toward the door, casting a murderous look at Marshal Hagan and saying, "You ought to be arrested yourself for hitting Custis from behind with your pistol!"

"He earned it," Hagan said dryly. "And Judge Klein won't be doing anything to help your friend. He's old and he's crusty and he doesn't like federal officers or officials any more than the rest of us in Prescott."

"We'll just see about that!" Laura shouted as she slammed the door in her wake.

Nurse Laura Danby headed for the territorial capitol building, and when she'd mounted its granite front steps, she went inside and found an armed guard seated at a desk. "Excuse me, can you tell me where I can find Judge Klein?"

"Home sick in his bed."

"And exactly where is that?"

The guard looked her up and down, not bothering to be subtle about his appreciation for the opposite sex, before saying, "Judge Klein lives about two blocks west of here. Big gray house with a nice front porch and white pillars. Got a little picket fence around it with daisies that his housemaid tends. You can't miss the place, but he won't see you when he's sick, and you don't want to see him when he's sick, either."

"I'll take my chances," Laura said in a clipped tone, heading back outside.

It took her less than ten minutes to find the house that the guard at the desk had described, but when she knocked on the front door, she was greeted by a large and stern-faced black woman.

"I need to see Judge Klein immediately."

"He is sick and can't be disturbed."

"But this is an *emergency*!"

The black woman folded her big arms across her massive breasts. "Come back in a few days and maybe the judge will be feelin' better."

Before Laura could form an argument, the door was slammed in her face. She knocked again and again. The door didn't open, and when she tried to turn the knob, she heard a deadbolt being slid shut.

"Dammit!" Laura cried, turning around and stomping back to the street. "What am I going to do now!"

She returned to the marshal's office, and Hagan wasn't any more helpful than he had been earlier. He smiled at her as if she were a stubborn child and said, "You look frazzled and weary from your travels."

"I'm just fine, thank you."

Hagan winked at her. "I'm thinking that you and the big man in my cell didn't sleep a lot coming out here from Denver. You need to go back to the hotel and rest for a few days until Judge Klein is able to take the bench and make a decision on this assault charge."

"And maybe you need to . . . Oh, never mind!" Laura said, managing to clamp her jaws shut tight before she said something very unladylike.

"Have a nice rest," Marshal Hagan told her. "Maybe a warm bath and some hot tea. Go to bed early and *alone* and try to get some sleep."

"Go straight to hell!" She charged past the man and marched off to Whiskey Row.

Longarm heard the door slam and it roused him to say, "Marshal Hagan, you really are getting way over your head on this one."

"I don't think so," the lawman replied. "You see, I'm very good friends with both Judge Klein and Governor Woodruff. So while you may believe that you have some big-shot connections with the federal authorities in Denver and maybe even Washington, D.C., I have the full support of the people who count in this new Arizona Territory."

"We'll see about that," Longarm told the man. "A day of reckoning will come for both you and Eli Pittman. It's not *if* it will happen, but when."

Marshal Hagan smiled, almost as if he had received a compliment instead of a threat. "I think I'll save the territory a bit of money and feed you bread and water until you go to court for sentencing. Bread and water always settles a prisoner down and puts him on his best behavior."

"You're a loathsome son of a bitch," Longarm told the lawman. "And it's going to be a real pleasure to mop the floor with you when the time comes."

"Don't hold your breath," Hagan replied as he poured himself a cup of his wretched coffee and opened a bag of freshly baked pastries.

Chapter 19

Nurse Laura Danby stood up at the end of her lengthy job interview and shook hands with Dr. Peter Jensen and Dr. George Pomeroy. Dr. Pomeroy was the older of the two physicians and probably the one who made the final hiring decisions, but Laura felt that the younger man, Dr. Jensen, would certainly have a strong say in the matter of her employment.

"There is one last question I forgot to ask," Dr. Pomeroy said as Laura was leaving the room.

"And that is?" she asked.

The older physician frowned and fidgeted a little, clearly uncomfortable with what he was about to ask. "Well, Miss Danby, I have heard that you just arrived in Prescott with a federal marshal who is now locked up in our jail. Is that true?"

Laura had been dreading this question. "It is true, Dr. Pomeroy. We came from Denver. Marshal Custis Long is on a manhunt and I was in some difficulty in Denver, so he was honorable enough to see that I had a safe journey to Prescott."

The two doctors exchanged quick glances, and Pomeroy said, "May I ask what kind of difficulty you were in back in Denver?"

She didn't hesitate to answer his question. "There was a doctor there who would not take no for an answer. He was a fine surgeon and practitioner of medicine, but in my case he became very . . . difficult. I'd really rather not discuss that sad relationship any further."

The younger doctor, whom Laura judged to be an eligible bachelor, gushed, "Of course not! What happened back there in regards to your personal life is none of our business."

"I'm glad that you feel that way," she said, hoping it was really true. "Thank you. Were there any more questions?"

The two men shook their heads and then the older doctor said, "Really, Nurse Danby, you have a remarkable résumé and medical background. I think when I talk to our board of directors that they will be genuinely enthused about you becoming the head of our nursing department. Most of our nurses have very little education or training and . . ."

Dr. Jensen quietly interrupted. "Miss Danby, there is one last question that I would like ask."

"Then please do."

"Are you in any way involved with the federal marshal and do you expect to remain here in our lovely territorial capital for an extended period of time?"

Nurse Danby took a deep breath and considered the two questions carefully, knowing that her answer would determine whether or not she was hired. "I am involved with Marshal Long, but only as a friend. He has protected me and assisted me greatly and I shall forever be in his debt. And as for my stay here in Prescott, from what I've seen of this lovely town, I think I will be staying for quite some time."

Dr. Jensen smiled broadly. "Excellent!" He turned to his older colleague. "Any more questions, Dr. Pomeroy?"

The older man barely concealed a smile. "Judging from your behavior, Dr. Jensen, I think not."

"Good!" Jensen said with relief. He took Nurse Danby's arm and escorted her out of the room and then the hospital. "I should like to personally deliver the news of our hiring decision. Perhaps over dinner this evening?"

"The decision will be made that soon?" Laura asked.

"If I have anything to do with it . . . yes."

"Then I'd love to have dinner with you and it has been a pleasure to meet you, Dr. Jensen."

"Peter. I'd rather you called me Peter when we are not in the hospital."

"Whatever you prefer."

"Miss Danby, your employment as head of nursing will dramatically upgrade our staff. And I promise you that whatever happened in Denver regarding that doctor who was . . . was difficult . . . well, it will not happen here."

"I'm very glad to hear that," Laura said, giving the man her most radiant smile and then leaving with a little extra sway in her shapely hips. Dr. Peter Jensen wasn't as handsome and most certainly not as wealthy as Dr. Robert Gaylord, but he was modest and no doubt a much finer man. And while Dr. Jensen had none of Custis

Long's animal magnetism, he was really quite good-looking in his own sweet way.

Yes, Laura thought happily as she walked the tree-lined streets bordered with several fine Victorian homes, I do believe I could get to like living in Prescott very, very much.

"Miss Danby?"

Laura turned and saw a beautiful young woman about her own age and height standing on a corner. "Yes?"

"My name is Mrs. Rachel Pittman. I was hoping that I could have a few words with you in private."

Laura's smile faded and she thought, Now the real trouble begins. "Concerning?"

"Many things. Can I buy you a nice lunch so that we can enjoy our talk?"

Being low on funds and still waiting for her bank deposits to be forwarded to Arizona, Laura nodded. "Sure, why not?"

They found a little café and a small table in the back where the lunch crowd's conversation was not so deafening. Once their orders were taken, Rachel Pittman steepled her fingers and said, "I *know* why you and Marshal Custis Long are in Prescott."

"You do?"

"Yes. The United States marshal has come to kill my husband or arrest him and take him back to Denver."

Laura saw no sense in denying the fact. "And what do you know about me?"

"That you've just had an interview with Dr. Jensen and old Dr. Pomeroy and almost certainly will be hired as the head of the hospital's nursing staff."

Laura laughed out loud. "My goodness! You know

more about me than I know about me, it would seem."

"Not really. There is actually a lot I don't know but want to know, which is why we are here and having this conversation."

"Why don't you come right to the point," Laura suggested.

"All right. Marshal Custis Long doesn't seem like the kind of man who would come this far to just arrest Eli. And given the fact that my husband shot and nearly killed him and his boss, well, it's easy to come to the conclusion that either Marshal Long or my husband is not destined for old age."

"You are blunt," Laura said, sipping a tall glass of iced tea. "What do you really want? Because if you expect me to help your husband, then you've wasted money on this meal."

Rachel Pittman shook her head. "You don't understand at all, Nurse Danby. What I want to make sure of is that your big United States marshal *kills* Eli."

The glass of iced tea slipped out of Laura's hand and spilled on the table. She hardly noticed. "Good god, did I hear you correctly?"

"You did," Rachel told her. "Marrying Eli Pittman was the worst and most stupid mistake of my life. I've never regretted anything so much as I do that marriage. And now the easiest and safest thing for me would be to have your friend kill my husband so that I can move on with my life and finally be happy."

Laura shook her head. "I've never had a conversation with any person in my entire life such as this."

"Eli can be the most charming man in the world when he wants to be." Rachel told her. "He swept me off my feet and turned my head and heart like no man I've ever known. But once we were married and I was in his bed and under his control, the man became a monster. And he is terribly jealous and possessive."

"I believe you."

The waiter brought their food, and there were several minutes of silence as both considered what had been shared. Finally, Laura said, "What can I do to help you without being a part of a killing?"

"I'm sure that Marshal Hagan is keeping the federal officer in his jail so that he can have time to warn Eli that trouble is coming in his direction. In fact, I'm quite sure that is why Deputy Joe Cotter left town early this morning."

"I see."

"If Deputy Cotter finds Eli and warns him, then the federal marshal will be riding into a trap that he couldn't possibly survive."

"What do you want me to do?" Laura said.

"Marshal Hagan has had a lust for me since I was fifteen years old. He would do anything to . . . well, you know."

Laura was confused. "But what . . ."

Rachel leaned closer. "I'm going to go by the marshal's office and flirt with Marshal Hagan. Actually, I'm going to take a bottle of whiskey and *proposition* him."

"But . . ."

"Listen," Rachel whispered, "I'll get the marshal drunk. He's a heavy drinker, and I'll lure him out of the office and make sure that I drop the cell key just outside his door when we leave. You pick it up, free the big federal marshal, and tell him what I've told you."

"You're taking quite a risk," Laura said. "And what are you going to do with Marshal Hagan?"

"I'll take him out in the brush and get him so stinking drunk that he'll pass out cold."

"But he might attack and rape you!"

"I can take care of myself," Rachel said, reaching into her purse and extracting a derringer. "I'm sure that I won't have to use this, but I'm prepared to if I must."

"You are taking a terrible chance."

"If that federal marshal doesn't get out of jail and get to Eli before Deputy Joe Cotter finds him, I stand to lose everything I want or will ever need."

Laura thought about this for a moment and said, "All right. When are you going to visit Marshal Hagan and lure him out of the office?"

Rachel Pittman took a deep breath. "I'm going to prepare myself and then find a bottle to take to the man. I'll go to his office in about two hours. By late afternoon he will be drunk and we'll be sneaking out into the bushes. Will you watch for when we leave and I drop the key?"

"I'll watch and I'll be ready to free Custis Long."

"Is that his name?"

"Yes."

Rachel looked a little frightened, but she smiled anyway. "Tell him I think he is about the handsomest man I've seen in ages. Tell him that he has to kill my husband or I'm a dead woman and so is the man I love."

"I'll tell him that," Laura promised, "but believe me Custis already has plenty of motivation to kill Eli Pittman. He killed his brother only a few days ago at the Pittman Ranch."

"He killed Elias!"

"That's right," Laura said.

"Oh, thank gawd! Elias was almost as evil as his brother."

"Well," Laura said, "it's like you said before. When Custis finds Eli, only one of them will walk away from the fight. The only thing that worries me is that I've heard Eli has a bunch of Arizona Rangers around him down near the border."

"Don't you believe it," Rachel replied. "Governor Woodruff might have made him a captain, but the Rangers hate Eli and know he's rotten to the core. So when it comes to a showdown they won't interfere."

Laura sighed with relief. "That's about the best news I've heard in a long, long time."

Chapter 20

Longarm was dumbfounded when Rachel Pittman sashayed into the marshal's office with a bottle of whiskey and began to laugh and flirt with Hagan like some two-bit whore. At first, Marshal Hagan seemed a little nervous about having such a good time with a woman so young and beautiful, but after an hour or so of laughing, drinking, and carrying on, the lawman forgot all his inhibitions.

"My oh my," the marshal said. "And after all these years I thought you hardly knew who I was."

"Oh, honey," Rachel cooed, "I've looked up to and admired you since I was a teenage girl."

The fat marshal swallowed hard enough so that even Longarm could hear him gulp. "You did?"

"Why sure! I remember when you rode out with a posse and caught that stagecoach robber and two of his dangerous gang."

"Well, they actually weren't that dangerous," Hagan admitted. "It was just some poor farmer and his two sons.

They were havin' such a tough time of it they figured that they had no choice but to try to steal money."

"Oh, I hardly believe that they were all that harmless, Marshal. They were armed, weren't they?"

"Yeah, but the farmer admitted his gun wasn't safe to fire and the two boys just had slingshots."

"Never you mind," Rachel said. "It took a lot of courage to go after those three."

"Yeah," Hagan said, "I reckon it did at that. You get hit with a rock from a slingshot, it could brain you!"

"Why, of course it could! You really are a very, very brave man."

Longarm just shook his head in amazement as he lay on his bunk and pretended to be asleep while the pair laughed and giggled. But when Rachel said, "Why don't we go somewhere where we can be alone for a little while?" Longarm began to get the picture.

"Well," Hagan gulped, practically drooling all over the front of his shirt, "I shouldn't really do that."

"Your choice," Rachel said. "But my husband is away and I'm feeling sort of . . . well, itchy and twitchy . . . if you know what I mean."

The marshal giggled, and his fat belly jiggled with excitement and anticipation. "Well," he croaked, "I guess we could go for a little walk out back. It won't take me very long to show you what I can do for a pretty young thing like yourself."

"Oh," Rachel crooned, "it might take a longer than you think."

Longarm rolled his head to watch Marshal Hagan practically fall out of his desk chair in his haste to leave the office and race around back into the bushes. As

Hagan was fumbling for his keys, Rachel turned and gave Longarm a wink and a wave.

Longarm grinned back at her and gave her a thumbs-up.

Not three minutes later, Laura stepped through the door with the keys to his cell dangling in her hand. "Hi, Custis! Interested in going for a little ride today?"

"Any place but this cell looks good. How did Mrs. Pittman do with Marshal Hagan?"

"She put the poor man into such a state I doubt he knows if he is coming or going."

"I saw that much," Longarm told her. "But what is the woman going to do with the marshal if he gets rough?"

"Don't you worry about Rachel," Laura assured him. "I can tell you right now that she is a woman who knows how to handle men, and she isn't going to be shy about pulling her derringer out and making her point if Hagan starts to acting too randy."

Longarm stepped out of the jail cell and immediately went to get his badge, pocket watch, gun, and rifle. "Why is Rachel Pittman helping me?"

"Because she wants you to kill her husband before he finds out that she has found another lover."

"She wants me to kill Eli?"

"That's right."

Longarm snorted. "She really is quite a woman!"

"So you think so?"

"But not as pretty as you," Longarm added quickly as he strapped on his gunbelt.

The truth of it was that Rachel had excited him with her bold advances on the older marshal, even if he did know that they had been feigned. Rachel was so good-looking and . . . well, sexually stimulating . . . that he almost felt sorry for Hagan because the man had been like a lamb being led to the slaughter.

"I didn't have time to get our horses ready," Laura said, following Longarm out the door and then locking it and tossing the keys into a nearby horse trough. "But I doubt it will take very long for us to get out of Prescott."

Longarm's mind was focused on leaving, and he walked swiftly along with his head down, making Laura half run to keep up with him on the way to the livery stable.

A half hour later they were in the saddle and Laura was telling him what he already knew, and that was that Captain Eli Pittman was somewhere down along the Mexican border.

"How far away do you think that is?"

"Long damn way," he said, knowing how hard that many miles would be on Laura.

"Custis, is it a lot more than a day's ride?"

"I'm afraid so. It might take three or four days, and the riding is going to be hot and hard."

Laura hauled her horse to a standstill. "Wait!"

Longarm reined in and turned his horse around to wait for her to trot up beside him. "What?"

Laura leaned forward and patted her mount's neck. "You know how you didn't want me to leave Flagstaff, but when I did, I helped you at the Pittman Ranch?"

"Sure. I doubt I could have gotten out of that fix without your help," Longarm said truthfully.

"And aren't you glad that I came down here to Prescott and helped you escape the jail just a little while ago?"

"Again, I couldn't have done it without your help and that of Mrs. Pittman."

"Well," Laura continued, "I'm afraid that I can't help you anymore. You see, I've taken a job at the Prescott hospital, and I just don't think I am physically able to ride for three or four hard and hot days. What I'm saying, Custis, is that I no longer believe that I can be of much help to you."

Longarm was surprised but not disappointed by her decision. "I understand completely. The ride from Flagstaff to Prescott is a cakewalk compared to the trail I'm about to take down to the border. And even when I get there, it's going to be tough going. So I'm glad that you're turning back, and congratulations on your new job."

"I'm going to be the head of their nursing department," Laura told him proudly. "They don't have anyone nearly as well qualified, and I think that I made a very good impression on the two doctors who interviewed me for the position. Especially Dr. Jensen."

Longarm chuckled. "Don't tell me . . . let me guess. Dr. Jensen is young and a bachelor."

"Right."

"Is he also handsome and rich like that asshole back in Denver, Dr. Gaylord?"

"Afraid not," she said. "But he's . . . cute."

"And he's probably going to act like a puppy around you."

Laura laughed. "He might."

Longarm rode his horse up close to Laura, reached out, and pulled her a ways out of the saddle to plant a kiss on her lips. "I'm going to miss that, Nurse Danby. And a whole lot more."

"You'll have the señoritas climbing all over you down by the border and won't give the memory of me two minutes of your time."

"Not so," he said, meaning it. "And if you're not hooked up with that young Dr. Jensen when I return, I'm going to rope you and tie you spread-eagled across my hotel room bed."

"My, that sounds exciting!"

He stuck out his hand. "Thanks for helpin' me out twice, Nurse Danby. I'll be seeing you before long."

"Take good care of yourself," she said, blowing him a kiss as she wheeled her horse around and trotted back toward Prescott, which was still plain to see in the distance.

Laura rode into Prescott and right up along Whiskey Row. She tried not to laugh as she saw Marshal Hagan shouting and pounding on his door while a locksmith tried to get it open.

Marshal Hagan, it would appear, was going to have a devil of a time explaining how he got locked out of his own office and how his sole prisoner, a famed United States marshal, had escaped and locked the door behind him.

A horse came galloping up the street, and when Laura turned her attention away from the marshal and his problem, she caught just a glimpse of the rider in the passing.

It was Rachel Pittman, and for reasons only she would know, the woman was obviously chasing United States Marshal Custis Long south.

Chapter 21

Rachel considered herself an expert horsewoman, and the mare she was riding was a tall roan with both speed and endurance. She had a bedroll tied behind her saddle and a pair of saddlebags hooked over her saddle horn, along with two rawhide-bound canteens. Under her right leg was a rifle scabbard, and the Winchester it held was almost new. The Colt revolver resting against her shapely hip had been her father's favorite pistol, and Rachel had fired it since she was a child.

When she saw Longarm up ahead about noon, she drew the Colt, raised it into the air, and fired a single shot. Longarm reined about sharply and drew his own pistol, then waited until he recognized who was following him. Even then he kept the gun in his hand, not sure if the Pittman woman was a real friend or a cunning, seductive foe.

"What are you doing!" he demanded as she drew her roan mare up close to his gelding and let the animal catch its wind.

"I've come to help you kill my husband," Rachel said. "The way I see it, you're going to need some help, given that he shoots both fast and straight."

"So do I."

"I expect that you do," Rachel said. "But if you go alone and the trouble starts, Deputy Cotter will side with Eli and may even get the Arizona Rangers to go along with him. However, if I'm riding with you, they just might think twice since most of them owe their appointment to the governor."

Longarm stared at the beautiful woman. "What was that all about back at Marshal Hagan's jail?"

"I think you're smart enough to figure it out."

Longarm thumbed back the brim of his Stetson and scowled. "So this is all about you wanting me to kill your husband so that you can . . .?"

"Find a good man to marry . . . or maybe *not* to marry. But it's like I told your friend the nurse . . . I fear Eli. He has a violent streak a mile deep and two miles long, and someday he'll catch me humping a handsome gent and kill us both."

"I'll admit that's a heavy sword to have hanging over your head." Longarm hooked a knee around his saddle horn and shifted on the leather for a bit of comfort. "But I don't really think you believe you can be of much help when the shooting starts."

"Well you have another think coming, Marshal. See that little stump about thirty yards over there?" she said, pointing.

"Sure."

"Watch this." Rachel drew her pistol and fired in one

smooth motion that seemed unhurried but was amazingly fast.

"Wow!" Longarm said, not bothering to hide how impressed he was at her skill with a handgun. "Where did you learn to draw and shoot like that?"

"Take a guess."

"Eli taught you."

"That's right, Rachel said. "When we were courting, we often used to ride out of Prescott in a buggy with rifles and pistols when the weather permitted. We'd take a picnic and we'd screw on a blanket then shoot, screw then shoot. It got so I liked the shooting almost as much as the screwing."

If the situation hadn't been so serious, Longarm would have laughed out loud at the picture that instantly sprang to mind. Instead, he pointed to the rifle. "How good are you with that Winchester?"

"I'm even better than Eli."

"Talk is cheap, Mrs. Pittman."

"Don't ever call me that again!" she snapped in anger as she yanked the rifle out of her scabbard and her eyes searched for a good target. "See that little rock resting on the boulder about a hundred yards north?"

"Sure."

"Watch in envy," she said, stepping off her mare and handing him the reins.

Rachel didn't waste a motion as she levered a shell into the rifle, threw it to her shoulder, and fired using just a split second to aim. The small rock disintegrated in a cloud of dust. She handed the rifle to Longarm and said, "Let's see what you can do, Marshal."

"I can't shoot that good with a rifle," he said, "but I'm passable. See that long branch sticking off the top of that dead tree?"

"Which limb?"

"That one," Longarm said, aiming and firing.

The dead tree limb shattered and fell to the ground.

"That's pretty good shooting," she told him.

Longarm nodded. The truth was that he'd been lucky to hit the limb, but he wasn't going to admit the fact to this brazen woman from Prescott.

Rachel jammed the rifle into her scabbard and mounted the roan. "I know the way south better than you do."

"How can you know where Eli is at any given time?"

"Because he isn't chasing Mexican banditos like he'd have everyone believe."

"No?"

"Nope."

"Then what is he doing along the border?"

"Well," Rachel said, "I've never actually seen him down there, but I can pretty well guess what he is up to right now and for the next few weeks. He's rustling horses and cattle from the poor villages south of the border and driving them back into our country to sell. And he's also screwing a lot of Mexican girls and drinking buckets of tequila."

"For a fact?" Longarm said with surprise. "I mean, he's with the Arizona Rangers."

"They're not really Rangers. They're just a bunch of thieves that Eli helped get badges. The *real* Arizona Rangers would never let any of them join."

Longarm unhooked his leg and jammed his boot into

the stirrup. "Rachel," he said, "if what you've told me is true, you've just made my job a whole lot easier. The thing that I was most worried about was the Rangers."

"The men that ride and raid with my husband are no more than common cattle and horse thieves. They plunder, rape, and pillage. But don't you dare think this is going to be easy. We're up against some tough men, and Deputy Cotter is also very good with a gun."

Longarm considered all that this woman had told him, and he still had many unresolved questions in this mind. "Any chance that we could get some help along the way down to the border?"

"I have money," she said, patting one of her saddle-bags. "Quite a bit of money, and I don't mind spending it if we come upon some hard men that we think we can trust to stand and fight."

Longarm didn't like that idea. "That's not the way I do things. I don't hire gunmen to fight my battles."

"Of course you don't," Rachel said. "You want to do it all by yourself so you can go back to Denver and tell everyone how brave and deadly you were in Arizona. But I want my husband dead and I don't want to die in the process. So even if you don't agree with my method, I hope you will at least let me spend my money as I see fit."

"If you put it that way," Longarm told her, "I don't see how I could object. And do you have any grub bound up in that big bedroll?"

"I've got canned meat, crackers, and a couple of bottles of good whiskey. Coffee and a pot to boil it in and some beans and salt pork. How's that sound?"

Longarm laughed and stuck out his hand. "I think

you and I are going to ride the trail south as the best of friends."

"Maybe even more than that," she hinted. "Are you in love with that nurse from Denver?"

"More in lust," he sheepishly admitted.

"Lust is good, Marshal Long. Lust is real good. I have a question to ask you."

"Then ask it."

"The border stretches for hundreds of miles. What were you going to do to find Eli?"

"I heard from a fella in a saloon that your husband really enjoys a little town called Los Algodones that is right on the border not far south of Yuma."

"You're right. That's where he has his connections and where he operates. I'm glad to know that you weren't just going to work your way all the way over to Brownsville, Texas, on the Gulf of Mexico."

"Give me a little credit, Rachel. I haven't lasted this long as a federal marshal by being completely stupid."

"You don't look stupid at all," she said. "What you look like is a *stud*."

Her words put a wide grin on his face, and Longarm couldn't help but feel heat rising in his loins. But the day was still young and the night a long time coming, so he pushed lust from his mind, tugged his hat down tight, and put his gelding into an easy canter.

This was, he decided, going to be an even more interesting hunt than he'd expected.

Chapter 22

"This is one heck of a hot and ugly country," Longarm said on the second day of their ride. "Not good for much except rattlesnakes, scorpions, and Gila monsters."

"Buzzards do well here, too," Rachel told him. "Eli told me it was four days of hell to ride down to the border, and I always took his word on that. He figured it was about two hundred of the driest miles on this planet."

"I'm missin' my tall, cool Colorado Rockies," Longarm said, wiping sweat from his face. "And as I remember, the Apache are still raiding down in this part of the country."

"Yes," Rachel said, "but if we're lucky, we'll pass through all this rock, sage, and sand without being seen by Indians or banditos."

Longarm looked out at the desolate and seemingly endless expanse of broken rock and sage. "How many more of these damned sun-blasted mountain ranges are we going to have to cross, and do you know if there is any water up ahead?"

"I've only been down this way twice," Rachel admitted. "But I do recall where to find water. Right up ahead rising out of the heat waves are the Eagle Tail Mountains, and about fifty miles behind them are the Castle Dome Mountains. They all have a few springs. I'm hoping they haven't dried up this year."

"That would be a comfort," Longarm told her.

"Don't be sarcastic," she warned. "Eli was good at it, and I've got a thin skin when it comes to sarcasm."

"I'll bet you have a thin skin due to a lot of the things Eli did."

"Yeah," she said, "but he sure could pleasure a woman. Until I met him, I thought a man and a woman humping was about as fun as peeing in the morning."

"I never liked Eli," Longarm said. "When he came to Denver and my boss hired him, I knew it was a mistake."

"How did you know right away?"

"There was just something about the man that struck me as being wrong. He never even mentioned for a long, long time that he was married. Then when your territorial governor was wounded, Eli made a big deal of the fact that his wife was related to Governor Woodruff."

"And I'll bet Eli just had a grand old time with the Denver women," she said, not bothering to hide her bitterness.

"I heard that he did," Longarm said, deciding to be honest. "And there were a few times I saw him with different women."

"He attracted women to him like flies to honey, only there wasn't anything sweet about Eli once you got below his skin." She slapped and killed a big horsefly that had landed on her mare's neck. "Eli was kinda like that fly I just swatted. He was always after your blood."

"That bad?"

"You ought to know. And why I didn't see the *real* man at first is something that I have never understood."

Longarm chuckled. "It had to be that lust thing we talked about."

"I know," she admitted, "but a woman ought to have better sense."

"Don't be so hard on yourself, Rachel. A lot of women have thrown their lives away on worthless men and a lot of men have done the same thing over bad women."

She cast him a sideways glance. "Custis, I'll bet you never made a fool out of yourself over a woman."

"Oh, I've done that a time or two . . . but I never married 'em."

"You got something against marriage?"

"Yeah," he answered, "I don't like the commitment and I don't enjoy babies, toddlers, or even small kids."

"Maybe it would be different if they were *your* kids."

"I've given that some thought, but I don't think it would make any difference if they were mine or someone else's. I just never have found 'em to be anything but selfish and self-centered little buggers."

"My," Rachel said, "you are an ogre!"

"I suppose that I am, but the picture I have of coming home every evening to the same grubby, whining little faces puts a bad taste in my mouth. But most of all, I don't think I'd make a good husband and I don't want to mess up some good woman's life."

Rachel had listened quietly, and now she said, "It

sounds like you've put quite a lot of thought into convincing yourself that your only choice is to remain a lifelong bachelor."

"I guess that I have. And finally, in my line of work, 'lifelong' might not be very long. I've seen the families of good lawmen who have died in the line of duty. Some of their widows remarry . . . if they're still young and not bad looking . . . but a lot of them are left with a mortgage they can't pay and kids they can't even afford to clothe or feed. I've seen them wind up as charity cases . . . their kids being sent to orphanages."

"That would be hell on earth for a woman."

"You bet. Once, a friend of mine who was shot to death making an arrest left his wife in such desperate straits that she took work first in a saloon, then the saloon's cribs out in the back alley. That poor widow lasted two years, and one cold morning they found her naked in an alley with a knife buried in her heart."

Rachel expelled a deep breath and shuddered, as if to dispel the image of the poor widow from her mind. "We both know the world can be cruel. I was always taught that a person had to learn to be self-sufficient. That they needed to master some skills so that they could make an honest living when things went bad, as they always do now and again for all of us."

"That was a good lesson to learn," Longarm told her. "And it's one that I was taught young as well."

"What would you do if you couldn't be a United States marshal?"

"I'd probably be a gunsmith or a Pinkerton agent. Maybe a locomotive engineer. I've always liked trains and thought that would be one hell of a fine life, just riding the rails day and night."

"I guess that would be a nice thing to do," she said. "I've not ridden a train very much. Never slept in a fancy sleeping car or dined on linen and had someone wait on me as the world flew past."

"It's a *great* way to travel," he said. "And if you ever come to Denver, you should give it a try."

"Maybe I'll come back to Denver with you after we kill Eli," she told him.

Longarm didn't quite know what to say about that, so he kept his mouth shut. Way up ahead he saw buzzards circling low. He pointed at them and said, "What do you make of that, Rachel?"

"Could be a dead horse, cow, or even just a coyote," she replied. "Then again it could be a man or woman. We're going to pass maybe two miles west of where those buzzards seem to be attracted."

"I think that we'd better change our course a mite and investigate," Longarm told her. "Just in case."

Twenty minutes later they came upon a dead horse. It was easy to see that the animal had fallen while running hard, because it had stepped into a hole and broken its foreleg. The rider would have been hurled to the earth, but he must have survived the fall, because he'd cut the suffering animal's throat.

"Cutting a thrashing horse's throat wouldn't have been easy," Rachel remarked. "Especially given how hard the rider must have been thrown while his horse was running."

"He did it to avoid having his gunshot heard by anyone who might want to bring him grief or death," Longarm told her.

"Well," Rachel said, "he failed in that regard. Look at
the tracks of the Indian ponies. You can see that after
milling around they headed south."

"The tracks don't look all that old," Longarm said. "I
wonder who . . ."

Rachel knew what Custis was thinking. "That dead
horse belongs to Deputy Pete Cotter."

Longarm said, "We're following at least four Indians.
Probably Apache, and it's plain that they're after Hagan's
deputy, who is most likely hurt and definitely on foot.
We've got about two hours left of daylight. I doubt we'll
overtake them before nightfall."

Rachel nodded. "Deputy Cotter is no good, but I don't
think we can just let the Apache capture and torture him
to death."

"I agree," Longarm said. "Let's just keep moving."

Rachel checked the Colt on her hip. "I was hoping
we'd have clear sailing down to Los Algodones. But then
this is typical of how my life has gone these last few
years. Things just don't come easy for me anymore."

"They never did come easy for me," Longarm told
her. "Let's push these horses into a trot and try to make
up some ground on the Indians and Deputy Cotter."

"Okay," she said, "but if we aren't careful in this fad-
ing light our own horses might step into a hole, and we'll
wind up in the same terrible fix as Hagan's deputy."

"Point well taken," Longarm said, his eyes squinting
against the harshness of the lowering western sun.

Chapter 23

Longarm and Rachel rode by moonlight for two hours, and when a cloud passed across the face of the half moon and visibility was almost completely gone, they made a dry camp in an arroyo mostly filled with tumbleweeds. The stars were as brilliant as a field of diamonds tossed upon a jeweler's black velvet cloth. Longarm and Rachel were tired and had little to say to each other, but just as they were about to fall asleep, they heard the ragged rattle of distant gunfire.

"Six pistol shots," Longarm counted.

"No rifle shots?"

"The deputy's rifle was pinned under his dead horse when it fell and that's why Cotter couldn't get it. But the Indians were able to pull the horse over and retrieve that rifle."

"I didn't see the signs of that," Rachel confessed. "So do you think that Pete Cotter is dead?"

"Not necessarily," Longarm told her. "He might have a bunch of extra bullets in a cartridge belt, and maybe he found some high rocks or a good defensive position."

Even as Longarm was saying this, they heard more scattered gunfire. This time the firing was slower, which told them that either the Indians had overrun Cotter and taken his weapon, or they had a few handguns of their own and were not wasting precious bullets.

"What do you think?" Rachel asked anxiously.

"I'd guess that the gunfire is coming from about two miles away."

Rachel touched Longarm and asked, "Should we go and see if we can help the man? Otherwise . . ."

Longarm had been struggling with that question for the past hour and had reached a decision. "Cotter is probably already dead or dying. If we go barging in on the Apache in the dark, we'll get ourselves shot up and probably killed."

"But to just sit here while the deputy is fighting for his life . . ."

"Rachel, your life is far more important to me than that of Deputy Cotter. We ought to try to get there at sunrise, and if the deputy is still alive . . . maybe holed up where the Apache or whoever is after him can't easily reach him . . . then we'll do what we can to help."

"Sunrise," she said, lying back down on her blanket. "All right. But one thing you should know, and that is that if we save Deputy Cotter, he might try to kill you later."

Longarm saw a shooting star and hoped it was a good omen. "So you're telling me Cotter won't be forever grateful?"

"That's right."

Longarm heard another gunshot, then nothing. He

wasn't eager to jump into a fight with four Apache and maybe a few more that had joined their band. On the other hand, he wasn't able to just turn his back on a man facing long odds to save himself from what would most likely be a gruesome and protracted death. This was a difficult moral dilemma, and as he laid his head down on his saddle, Longarm wondered if he was even going to be able to catch a few hours of badly needed sleep.

They awoke well before dawn, stiff and cold because the desert was a land of extreme temperatures that varied widely between the nights and days. Having saddled their horses and tied the bedroll behind Rachel's cantle, they mounted up and silently rode south, watching the first pale light of the sun peek over the eastern horizon.

"Let's not skylight ourselves," Longarm told her as he guided his buckskin through the dry washes and kept to the low sides of the brushy hills.

"What are we going to do when we come upon them?" she asked.

"I have no idea," Longarm replied. "We'll just have to play this however the string runs out."

She didn't seem very much impressed with his answer. "I would have thought that someone with all your experience would have figured out a real *plan*."

"In situations like this, plans never work. How can we plan anything when we don't know what we're riding into?"

Suddenly, they heard a frantic burst of gunfire, then what had to be Cotter's wild and terrified screams.

A last gunshot and an ominous silence.

Longarm drew his horse to a standstill and bowed his

head. "It's over," he said. "And given as how other Apache might have joined the four that took up the hunt, I think we'd better just lay low and hope that the deputy died quickly."

Rachel expelled a deep breath. "It sounded as if he did."

"Then Cotter must have saved a last bullet for himself."

Longarm and Rachel waited hidden for about an hour, and then they remounted and rode quietly out of hiding. Another tense thirty minutes passed before they saw the Indians galloping way to the east, already mere specks on the horizon, each kicking up little puffs of dust.

Deputy Joe Cotter was dead, and his naked body had suffered horrible mutilations. Longarm dismounted and handed his reins to Rachel. "There's no reason for you to have this weighing on your mind. Just ride off a ways and let the horses eat whatever they can find. I'll cover the body with rocks to try to keep the coyotes off it for a while."

"Joe Cotter was a bastard and he'd killed some people that shouldn't have died," Rachel said to no one in particular. "But he didn't deserve this kind of ending."

"Well," Longarm said, "if it's any consolation to you, he robbed the Apache of some sick pleasure. That was about the only thing he had in his power to do."

"I know."

"Move away then and let me get busy with this ugly business."

"I know of a spring not far from here."

"A spring would be nice as long as it isn't the one that those Apache were heading for."

"They were going in a different direction," she told him. "The spring I remember is just to the west of us about a half mile."

"I'll be along directly," Longarm told her. "It'll be good to have some cool, clean water."

"Who said it would be cool and clean?"

Longarm didn't answer. He was staring at the inhuman remains that had once been a man. Now all he wanted was to finish this grisly business and get to Los Algodones so he could kill Eli Pittman and finally turn his sunburned face toward Colorado.

Less than an hour later he was at the spring dunking his head into the water and slaking a big thirst. There had once been some cottonwoods near the water, but they'd long ago been chopped down for firewood. Even so, the spring was about seventy feet across and rimmed with short grass and willows. "Rachel, this is a really nice spring," he said, sitting back on his haunches and surveying his surroundings. "I expect that both men and animals come for many miles around to drink here."

"Look," she said, pointing. "Mustangs!"

There were six of them, and the stallion was a sorrel horse, big-necked, defiant, and yet extremely wary. Longarm watched him with his small band. "That's a fine animal. I'll bet he's been chased many a time and obviously never been caught."

"Probably like you with women, huh?" Rachel said,

washing her face and then removing her blouse to wipe her upper body with a handkerchief.

It was early and still pleasantly cool, but Longarm knew that would all change in a few hours. And he was trying hard not to remember how terrible Deputy Pete Cotter's body had been chopped up and desecrated with urine. Longarm would never understand why the Apache tortured and treated their captives so badly, but maybe they'd had their own people done even worse by Americans and Mexicans. Maybe it was just an eye for an eye . . . but it was hard to witness.

"It's really bothering you, isn't it?" Rachel said.

He pulled his eyes up from her large, luscious breasts. "What did you say?"

"I said what they did to Joe is really eating at you inside."

"I've seen a lot of death, but that doesn't mean it gets any easier." Longarm studied Rachel's body. "Looking at you helps plenty, though."

She sat back and pushed out her bare chest a little for his enjoyment. "You like what you see?"

"A man would have to be dead not to."

Rachel glanced up at the sky. "I wish we could stay here and rest a day or two. I'm afraid of what awaits us on the border."

"I promise you that we'll handle Eli and whoever else is willing to stand with him."

"I wish I was as confident as you are about that."

Longarm shrugged. "I'll admit that it could go bad for us . . . I'd be a fool not to realize that . . . but I've always expected to win my fights, and I see no sense in changing my attitude now."

"I'm just not as brave as you are, Custis."

"Naw. I don't believe that for a second. You're plenty brave or else you wouldn't have come after me. You could have stayed in Prescott. No one forced you into this."

She began to wipe the sweat from her breasts. "I figured that sooner or later Eli would return to Prescott, and then he'd either rape or kill me. I liked my chances with you."

"You ought to put that blouse back on," Longarm said, swallowing a knot in his throat. "I'm tired, but I'm still pumping red blood."

"Maybe you'd like to pump more than . . . red blood."

He almost laughed. "Are you suggesting that we couple right out here in hell's kitchen?"

She tossed her hair seductively. "If we must soon die, I'd like to think that we had made love at least once. And even if we do come out of this alive and intact, you might spot some little señorita down there that is about ten years younger than me and far prettier. If that happened, you'd decide I don't look so good after all."

"Never gonna happen, Rachel." He moved over beside her and kissed her lips, then began to stroke her breasts and nuzzle her big nipples. "And maybe we should stay here today and rest up the horses."

She laid her hand on his crotch and began to tickle what was growing with a fingertip. "That's really not a bad idea."

"I thought you might like it," he said, pushing her down on the grass and then removing her boots and lifting her riding skirt. "Nice legs."

"I'm glad you approve. If you like them, wait until you get to the next part of me."

Longarm smiled and stood up. He kicked off his boots, removed his gunbelt and then his hat, and unbuckled his pants. When he stepped out of them and his underwear, he spread his legs a little and stood over her very proud of what he had to show this woman.

"Good gracious!" Rachel exclaimed, "It's huge!"

"And it's stiff and ready to root."

Rachel pulled off the last of her underclothes, bent her knees a little, and said, "Come and get your fill, Big Boy!"

Longarm had hoped this might happen down in Los Algodones . . . if they survived. Now it was going to happen no matter what awaited them down on the bloody border.

He dropped to his own knees, bent, and then thrust his hips forward powerfully. Rachel groaned with pleasure, wrapped her legs around his waist, and pulled him deeply into herself.

"I love to ride horses," she whispered in his ear as he began to churn her honey pot, "but even more I love a man to ride me."

"Well," Longarm grunted, feeling powerful and lusty, "that's the best news I've heard all week."

He took her hard and fast the first time. Pushed her pulsating butt through the thin grass right down into the mud, and she howled like a coyote into the bright blue sky. Not so long afterward, they threw off what was left of their garments, waded out into the cool springwater, and made love and enough splashing to set a bullfrog to croaking.

Longarm and Rachel forgot about the hard desert that surrounded them for hundreds of miles in every direction.

They forgot about Eli Pittman and all the bad things that might be their fate down on the border. All they thought about was making love as often and as well as they had ever made love. And when night finally dropped on the desert, they didn't stop and they sure didn't give a damn that they got Rachel's bedroll all wet and sticky.

Chapter 24

Los Algodones, Mexico, was a small town about fifteen or twenty miles south of Yuma. It was a town where men went to forget about their past and refused to consider their bleak future. Prisoners from the notorious Yuma Territorial Prison often made a beeline to Los Algodones because it was the closest place to buy cheap liquor and more pretty señoritas than they could satisfy in their entire, wasted lifetimes.

Longarm and Rachel rode into the town late in the afternoon and found a large pole corral and brush-covered ramada where an old Mexican with a droopy straw hat was sipping tequila and lime juice. He spoke English passably well, and after only a few minutes, they left their horses, saddles, and other belongings with the old man, who assured that everything would be well guarded. And before leaving, they temporarily traded their Stetsons for droopy sombreros and colorful serapes. Looking a little more like the general populace, Longarm and Rachel headed up the dusty street mostly lined with noisy cantinas and street vendors selling chili peppers, tortillas, beans, corn, rice, tequila, and bitter dark beer.

"I'm hungry," Rachel said, heading toward two boys who were selling burritos. She was carrying their only rifle loosely in her right hand, for they had decided that Longarm would be faster and more accurate with his pistol.

Years before, Longarm had gotten food poisoning in Mexico, and he sure didn't want to repeat that experience, but he was also famished, and his belly won over his good judgment. He held up four fingers and pointed to the burritos. The boys grinned and put them together in no time at all, dousing everything with mouth-blistering hot salsa.

"*Gracias!*" they said in unison as Longarm paid them generously.

He and Rachel walked over to stand in the shade of a big ocotillo bush and then ate quietly, taking in the small but busy border town.

"So what if we see Eli come out of a cantina or a whorehouse?" Rachael asked.

"Then I'll throw down my food, bow my head so he doesn't recognize me, and try to move in close enough to get the drop on him."

"He won't surrender, and you have no authority here in Mexico."

"My Colt is my authority today, same as it is for anyone else. I doubt that there is even a constable in this lawless town. It's a shoot-first-and-ask-questions-later kind of place, and that suits me just fine."

Rachel ate quickly, the juice from the meat and salsa funneling down her chin and soaking into the serape.

Flies buzzed furiously around them and the heat was approaching ninety degrees.

"I sure don't want to die in a town like this," she said, finishing off her second burrito. "We're just a couple of gringos and I bet that nobody would even bother to bury us properly."

"Why don't we try to keep our minds off that sort of thing?" Longarm suggested, finishing his meal and wiping the grease from his face with the back of his bare arm. "I think we ought to just mosey around a bit and see if Eli is here or not."

"I know the horse that he rode out of Prescott on. It's a really handsome pinto gelding."

"That ought to be easy enough to catch our eye," Longarm remarked as he stepped out of the shade and slowly walked into the center of town, pretending to be mostly looking at the cantinas, as if he had a big thirst.

Rachel stayed close and they made an odd pair. Longarm was six-foot-three and Rachel was about a foot shorter. And even though she was wearing an oversized serape, you could still see that she had a pair of big melons on her chest. Longarm saw Mexicans studying them with half smiles and knew that they weren't fooling anyone into thinking they were just a pair of oddly matched locals.

"Keep your hair tucked up under your hat," Longarm said. "And keep your head down so that you don't draw a lot of attention."

"Do you really think that I can fool them into believing I'm a *man*? What about my chest?"

"It might help to slump your shoulders a little forward," he advised.

Rachel did such a ridiculous job of slumping forward that it was a struggle for Longarm not to grin at the sight of her attempting to look like a hump-backed little man. Several of the Mexicans who had been watching burst into gleeful laughter.

"Custis?

"Yeah?"

"The last time I was here, there was only one hotel in this place, and it's right up ahead on the left. If Eli and his bunch are in town, that's where we'll find them. There's a popular café and cantina inside that hotel and a couple of cribs out in back for the less desirable whores. The young and prettier ones service men upstairs all day and all night."

Longarm watched a fat Mexican woman waddle out of one of the cribs behind the hotel. She looked a little bit unsteady, and he decided she was probably drunk. She was singing in Spanish as she made her way toward an open latrine. When she got to it, she took great care to straddle the narrow latrine, then she lifted her colorful dress to take a dump and a piss. Her piss came down so hard it splashed her ankles, and she tried to spread her legs farther, lost her balance and nearly toppled. When she regained her balance and saw Longarm staring at her, she smiled and a gold tooth shone brightly in the sun. Gold tooth or not, she wasn't at all pretty, but Longarm had to admit that the gal could piss like a pony.

"There's a pinto tied to the hitching rail just up the street," Longarm said. "Does that look like it belongs to Eli?"

"I can't tell yet. Let's move closer."

They walked past the hotel, and when they neared the

pinto, Rachel shook her head. "That's a lot smaller horse than the one Eli rides. Not nearly as good an animal."

"Let's continue through town and then come back to the hotel," Longarm said. "I'm really hoping to get this showdown over with now."

They continued walking, sometimes stepping aside to make room for passing wagons. Once, a thin and tall spotted dog came out from under a porch. Its coat was splotchy and it appeared to have a severe skin disease. Even so, the animal tried to wag its tail and show that it was friendly and in need of food and sympathy.

"I'm sorry," Rachel said. "I don't have anything to give you, but I'll watch for you next time and have something."

"Watch for Eli or his pinto!" Longarm hissed. "And don't touch that dog or you might catch what it has and all your hair will fall out tonight."

"Then you wouldn't want to make love to me, huh?"

"Well, given how fresh it is in my mind what we did at the spring, and given that it would be dark, I might still be tempted to mount you."

"Selfish bastard," she whispered with a smile. "You men are all alike from the waist down."

"Keep looking and stay close," Longarm ordered.

"Everyone is staring at us," Rachel said. "Custis, it's obvious to me that we couldn't have attracted any more attention if we were strolling along here naked!"

"Oh, I wouldn't go that far."

"There," she said excitedly, almost throwing her arm up and pointing. "That looks to be Eli's pinto gelding. He loves that horse more than he ever loved me."

Longarm stopped and slowly pushed his serape up so

that the Colt revolver on his left hip would be easy to reach in a cross draw. "It's tied in front of a blacksmith's open-fronted shed. Let's go see if Eli is waiting inside to get his horse shod."

"Be very careful," Rachel warned. "You're much bigger than the average Mexican, and you stand out like a sore thumb. If Eli is inside the blacksmith's shed, he'll take a second and then a third look at you coming."

"And if he takes a third and sees your chest, we're really in trouble," Longarm added. "Just be ready with the rifle and don't get too close to me as we approach the horse."

Moments later, Rachel whispered, "This *is* Eli's pinto!"

Longarm stopped about fifty feet from the front of the blacksmith's shed. He could hear a hand forge being worked and the steady ring of an anvil. What was his next move going to be?

"Rachel, move away from me. Mosey over to the front of that shop. Have your rifle ready to shoot and then just wait while I make my way closer to the blacksmith's shed."

"Be *very* careful!"

Longarm slipped his hand closer to his gun butt. He knew that he was at a serious disadvantage because he was out in the sun while whoever was inside the blacksmith shop was partially hidden in shadow. If Eli Pittman had identified him, the man had probably already drawn his gun and was taking aim.

Sweat was beading out across Longarm's face and chest, and he changed his angle of direction so that he placed Eli's pinto directly between himself and the dim interior of the blacksmith's shed. If the shooting started, the pinto was going to be his shield, and that was a shame but something that could not be helped.

The sharp hammering ring stopped, as did the working of the bellows. Suddenly Longarm was aware of the buzzing of swarms of flies, the foot stomping of horses bothered by the flies, and the quick, light sound of bare running feet.

With the fine pinto between him and the now silent open shed, Longarm paused and drew his gun. "Eli?" he called. "Your time has run out. Give yourself up and I'll take you back to Denver to stand trial."

The droning of the flies seemed to grow louder.

"Eli, Billy Vail is *still alive*. You won't be hanged if you give yourself up."

Longarm heard a cough, or was it a laugh? "Well, Custis, you came a long, hot way to die in a dirty border town. You should have counted yourself lucky back in Denver and stayed there to get your retirement."

Longarm removed his sombrero and serape so that he was less encumbered. He glanced across the street to see Rachel crouched with the rifle ready in her white-knuckled hands.

"Come on out," Longarm ordered. "Last chance."

"Come and get me!"

Longarm took a deep breath. He signaled Rachel to stay exactly where she was and not to move.

"I'm coming," Longarm said tightly.

"I've got friends here in Los Algodones," Eli called. "Even if you get lucky now, they'll skin you like a rabbit and drag you through the streets before they throw you in the shit latrines, where the maggots will eat your rotting flesh!"

"We'll see."

"I'll let you go back to Denver," Eli called. "I let you live once, I'll give you the same chance *right now*."

Longarm untied the pinto, and staying behind the animal, he began to move slowly toward the blacksmith's open-fronted shed. Most men, even the worst, hated the idea of shooting a horse that they loved and admired. Maybe Eli would feel the same way about this pinto.

A shot blasted out of the dim interior, and Longarm heard a bullet whip-crack over the neck of the pinto. The animal heard it too and lunged forward in fear. The fingers of Longarm's left hand sank into the pinto's thick mane, and he was lifted off his feet. The horse was bucking toward the blacksmith shop, carrying him closer to Eli.

More gunshots and the pinto squealed in pain as Eli's second shot pierced its muzzle. The pinto went wild and began to rear and stomp. Longarm held on for a moment and then he was thrown ten feet, landing hard in the middle of the street. He rolled over and over toward an old wooden-wheeled caretta, as bullets traced his desperate progress toward cover. Eli Pittman jumped out into the sunlight and drew a second gun from his belt.

"Freeze!" he yelled as Longarm tried to roll and scramble for the cover of caretta two big wheels. Longarm had no intention of freezing and then being shot like a dying dog.

He raised his gun and fired at Eli, but there was dust and sweat in his eyes, and he was aware that one of Eli's bullets had sliced across his ribs and flatted against his belt buckle.

Eli crouched and took aim only thirty feet away. "So

long, Custis. The latrine shit-maggots will have you to-day for their dessert!"

Rachel had a clear shot, and she had no intention of merely wounding her husband so that he could live to go to prison and then one day return to exact his murderous vengeance.

"Eli!" she called, throwing off her sombrero and shaking out her long hair.

His head turned at the familiar sound of her voice. "Rachel?" Eli stared in amazement and blinked an instant before her rifle bullet struck him between the eyes and blew out the back of his head.

"Custis!" she shouted, racing across the street.

"I'm going to be all right," he said as she dropped in the dust to cradle his head in her lap.

"We'll find a doctor," she said, placing a hand over the bloody crease across his ribs.

"I have a whole lot better idea," he told her. "Let's find a bottle of tequila and get out of Los Algodones before Eli's friends come around looking for revenge."

"He doesn't have any friends . . . never did. No one will come after us. They're all just thieves and cowards."

Longarm climbed to his feet, and with Rachel's help, he staggered over to Eli's body, which looked a whole lot better than Pete Cotter's mutilated corpse.

"That was one hell of a fine shot, Rachel. Now check his pockets. Collect his gun and whatever else he has of value on him," Longarm said.

Rachel bent down, and with steady hands she went through her husband's pockets. "Two hundred dollars or more in cash. Some pesos and six silver dollars," she said in a quiet voice. "And this."

She extracted Eli Pittman's United States marshal's badge from his pocket, saying, "It's polished as bright as a diamond. I never knew him to take care of anything other than his gun."

Longarm accepted the badge and slipped it into his own pocket. "Maybe in some way he still valued that badge."

Mexicans had begun to emerge from the shacks and from the cantinas. Longarm saw one wearing a blacksmith's apron. He motioned the man over to them and pointed down at Eli, and then he pointed to the latrine.

The blacksmith backed away, his face reflecting horror and revulsion. Longarm relented. He pointed to the end of town and a small cemetery, then he made a motion as if he had a shovel in his hands.

The blacksmith and some of the other Mexicans understood and nodded in agreement. Longarm gave the Mexicans the six silver dollars, making it clear that they were being paid to bury Eli Pittman.

"What about the pinto?" he asked Rachel.

She walked over to the animal, whose head was low, and saw the slow drops of blood dripping into the dust of the street. Longarm followed her. "Do you want this horse or shall we leave it?"

"I loved this horse, hated the man who rode him."

Longarm examined the horse's bullet wound. "I think he'll be fine. I can get some wadding packed with grease, and if we take our time and don't push him too hard, he'll easily make it back to Prescott."

Rachel said, "Custis, let's spend a few days resting at the spring. It'll give you and the pinto some time to heal."

Longarm's lips formed into a slow smile. "I think that's

a great idea. But too much rest can be tedious to a man like me."

"I didn't say that *all* we'd do is rest." She lifted up on her toes and kissed his mouth. "I can think of plenty of other things we can do to keep ourselves busy."

Longarm accepted a towel from a pretty young Mexican woman, and she motioned him to press it to his side to stanch the trickle of blood from his bullet wound.

Longarm smiled and said, "*Gracias, señorita.*"

She spat on Eli's body, kicked it with all of her anger and might, and proudly replied, "*Por nada, hombre.*"

Watch for

**LONGARM AND THE HORSEWOMEN
OF THE APOCALYPSE**

the 394th novel in the exciting LONGARM
series from Jove

Coming in September!

GIANT-SIZED ADVENTURE FROM AVENGING ANGEL LONGARM.

BY TABOR EVANS

2006 Giant Edition:

LONGARM AND THE OUTLAW EMPRESS

2007 Giant Edition:

LONGARM AND THE GOLDEN EAGLE SHOOT-OUT

2008 Giant Edition:

LONGARM AND THE VALLEY OF SKULLS

2009 Giant Edition:

LONGARM AND THE LONE STAR TRACKDOWN

2010 Giant Edition:

LONGARM AND THE RAILROAD WAR

penguin.com/actionwesterns

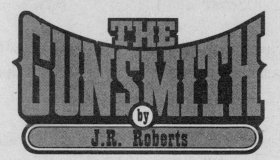
M11G0610